# The Terror of Fu Manchu

# The Terror of
Fu Manchu

by
William Patrick Maynard

A Black Coat Press Book

*In memory of Arthur Henry Ward and Cay Van Ash.*

*This book is dedicated to my loving wife, Steffanie and to our family: Steven, Michelle, Alexandra, Michael and Annie.*

Text copyright © 2009 William Patrick Maynard. All Rights Reserved.
Cover illustration copyright © 2009 Christine Clavel.

The character Fu Manchu and other characters from the works of Sax Rohmer are used by permission of The Society of Authors and the Authors League of America, Inc., owners of the copyrights in those works.

Visit our website at www.blackcoatpress.com

ISBN 978-1-934543-71-9. First Printing. April 2009. Published by Black Coat Press, an imprint of Hollywood Comics.com, LLC, P.O. Box 17270, Encino, CA 91416. All rights reserved. Except for review purposes, no part of this book may be reproduced or transmitted in any form or by any means, electronic or mechanical, including photocopying, recording, or by any information storage and retrieval system, without permission in writing from the publisher. The stories and characters depicted in this novel are entirely fictional. Printed in the United States of America.

## *Acknowledgements*

This book would not exist without the help of a great number of friends and acquaintances: John Ettinger of The Diogenes Club for suggesting that I write a Fu Manchu book back in October 2000; Dr. Lawrence Knapp for the wealth of research information on Sax Rohmer and his works available online at *The Page of Fu Manchu* website; Jeremy Crow of The Society of Authors for first entrusting me with Sax Rohmer's characters back in August 2002 (when this book was to be called *Shadow From the East: A Fu Manchu Thriller)* and for patiently waiting for me to get it finished and published; the late Richard Valley, editor and publisher of *Scarlet Street,* for his unfailing enthusiasm for this project from the beginning (thank you, Richard for your suggestion in August 2004 to develop Aziz); Michael Larsen and Elizabeth Pomada for their interest in the property and for having the wisdom in December 2006 to tell me to go back and start from scratch; Peter Rubie for his generosity in taking me under his wing and guiding me through rewriting the manuscript for the following eighteen months; Mrs. Rita Mills for her hospitality, her extensive research library, and her colorful anecdotes – one of which I shamelessly appropriated for this book; Steve Lewis for providing me with a complete set of Dr. Robert E. Briney's outstanding publication, *The Rohmer Review*; Len and Nora Peralta of *Jawbone Radio* for showcasing this project back in July 2006; Mike and Laura Schmidt for the kind use of The Empty Room; Zev Braun, Harry Long, Charles Prepolec, and Tom Amorisi for their support; Albert T. Longden for his willingness to work as a team; Manie Barron for trying his best to land this book with a major and for showing integrity from beginning to end; Jean-Marc Lofficier for throwing me a lifeline and being an honest partner; Edith May Hicks for first telling me about Fu Manchu nearly forty years ago; "Tulsa Blackie" for inspiring me to be a writer and whose version of the Frog and the Scorpion parable I borrowed for this story; most of all, thanks are due to my wife, Steffanie for believing in me and for sacrificing so much to allow me to complete this book.

W.P.M.

## *Foreword*

Dr. Fu Manchu, the brilliant criminal mastermind, first appeared in "The Zayat Kiss," an engaging mixture of British detective fiction and supernatural horror that graced the pages of *The Story-Teller* in October 1912 to instant acclaim. The honorable, but deadly, Chinese doctor personified, transcended, and (arguably) went a long way towards rehabilitating the racist stereotype of "the Yellow Peril" that followed in the wake of the Boxer Uprising—the international conflict that ushered in the dawn of the 20th century. Arthur Ward, under the *nom de plume* of Sax Rohmer, would author a total of 13 bestselling novels featuring the character from 1913 to 1959, as well as a posthumous collection of short fiction. Rohmer, a prolific author, playwright, songwriter, poet, comedy sketch writer, biographer, occultist, and amateur Egyptologist, was never able to escape the shadow of Fu Manchu as far as the public was concerned. The character became the subject of dozens of films, radio series, television series, newspaper strips, and comic books.

Rohmer's long-time assistant, Cay Van Ash (who co-authored the only book-length biography of Rohmer with the late author's widow), carried on the tradition by penning two further period Fu Manchu thrillers in the 1980s (a third was just underway when Van Ash passed away in 1994). *The Terror of Fu Manchu* marks the first authorized appearance of Sax Rohmer's classic pulp characters in book form in over 20 years. Shortly before his death, Rohmer stated that, while he would one day be forgotten, Dr. Fu Manchu would live forever. The original 14 Rohmer titles are on the verge of being rediscovered by a new generation of readers through an ambitious reprint campaign. As classic Rohmer and new period Fu Manchu thrillers find a place on readers' bookshelves, can it be very long before the Devil Doctor finds his way to the 21st century? Readers would do well to recall the stylish ending of the 1960s film series when Christopher Lee's voice would ring out in movie theaters with Fu Manchu's ominous threat that "the world shall hear from me again."

Finally, the following novel makes use of language that, while in keeping with the period, may prove unsettling to modern readers. For example, the word *Chinaman* was used most commonly to describe Chinese people the same way *Englishman* was used to describe the British. The word has since taken on a derogatory meaning and, indeed, such use of *Chinaman* and other stereotypical descriptors is also found in a book set in a less-enlightened day that deals directly with racial and cultural prejudices. We trust the modern reader can set aside their own reactions to such language and appreciate their use in the context of the story as well as understanding the author's intent in highlighting such views rather than sugar-coating the era being depicted.

W.P.M.

## 1. SHADOW FROM THE PAST

*I was running for my life. My heart was pounding furiously. The tendons in my legs felt ready to tear as I pushed myself harder and harder. My eyes stung with sweat. The wind rushed in my ears. The only sound that registered was the snapping of branches. The path through the dense foliage was starting to lead rapidly downhill. I took in great gulps of air as the force of the downward slope carried me into a group of low-hanging trees.*

*The incessant chattering of my pursuers suddenly drowned out all other noise. Some of them were following on foot while others swung apelike through the trees. I was oblivious to the branches that scraped against my limbs and torso. The bloody gashes they left would not slow me. Hesitation would mean certain death with those fiends on my trail.*

*My knees buckled and I tumbled and rolled. I tried to curl myself into a ball to protect my face from the twigs and stones as I neared the bottom of the hill. The chattering in the air had given way to excited guttural outbursts.*

*They had me! Those devils knew they had me!*

*I twisted and felt my back arch. I did not want to die screaming as a jagged blade sawed through my neck. I begged Christ Almighty to keep Freda and our little girl safe. I covered my head with my hands as I sunk waist-deep into the thick, cold mud. Panting with excitement, my pursuers gathered round to block all chance of escape.*

*Misshapen, brutish arms reached out and dragged me from the mud.*

*Blinded with fear and rage, I mustered what little strength remained and managed to propel myself into their midst. Biting and gouging, I threw my weight into them. I lashed about from one side to the next as my fingers grasped for eye sockets and nostrils. I ripped and tore with an animal ferocity. I had to stop myself from choking as I bit hard and deep into the warm, fleshy neck of the fiend nearest me.*

*I was growling savagely as I wrested the axe from his slimy yellow hands and swung it in a blinding arc as low as my arms would stretch. The devil's contorted features froze in fear. Time seemed to stop as I watched my hands quickly turn the axe over and use the blunt end to wrench flailing intestines from the gaping hole I had carved in his stomach.*

*The savages seemed to know fear for the first time since the atrocities had begun. I pressed forward swinging the axe with precision, cleaving skulls and limbs as if they were overgrown hedges. One after another of those filthy savages fell wailing as I exacted merciless revenge for the scores of Christian men, women, and children they had slaughtered these past few weeks.*

*It was over within minutes. I alone stood amidst the carnage. The mud had turned crimson with the blood of my enemies. I was gasping for air. My sense of smell seemed heightened by the odor of death. I looked around at the bodies of my vanquished foes, but I did not see the bestial yellow demons that had pursued me so relentlessly through the jungle. The bloodied corpses that lay at my feet belonged only to men.*

*"God in Heaven, what have I done?"*

*I looked up in despair and knew only Darkness.*

## 2. COURTING DISASTER

"Good Heavens!"

I exclaimed as I looked up from the manuscript on the table before me and into the eyes of its author.

"I must admit that you paint the Boxer Uprising in disturbing detail. Frankly, I cannot imagine anyone wanting to read a tale quite as shocking as this one."

"Then, one would be forgiven for mistaking you for the novice author, Dr. Petrie, as I can assure you there is no shortage of readers for such bloodthirsty prose."

Eltham laughed nervously as I handed his manuscript back to him.

"Still...I wouldn't want you to think that the whole book is quite as intense as the bit you just read. It is largely the story of one man's quest for spiritual truth, as anyone who remembers my name would have reason to suspect. Of course, if I know McBride, he will try and carve out the reflective passages leaving only the nasty bits to satisfy the ever-coarsening public appetite."

I grimaced as I considered the fact that, if the public's tolerance for such lurid portrayals of wanton savagery really had grown insatiable, then it was thanks, in no small part, to the avid following garnered by my continuing account of the secret war being waged against the British Empire by the diabolical Dr. Fu Manchu and his minions.

My host for this evening was John Daniel Eltham, a man who had achieved no small measure of notoriety as

Parson Dan during the Boxer Uprising. He had been merely Reverend Eltham when Nayland Smith and I had first met him more than a decade after those awful days. It was difficult to reconcile the quiet, unassuming churchman so fond of his gardening that we had first met with the fiery, intolerant zealot who had done so much to incite the Boxers against the West during his missionary years. Now, I found myself becoming acquainted with still another incarnation of the man as J. D. Eltham had recently left the ministry and was about to re-invent himself as an author.

It was a decision that allowed him to confront his past rather than leave it sleeping, as it had done for so many years, with the memory of the wife who had fallen victim to the same terrible conflict. Most surprising of all was Eltham's willingness to bring these events to light with the pending publication of his memoirs. The book was one certain to cause a public sensation and would likely open more than a few old wounds. Leave it to a Churchman, even a former Churchman, not to know when to leave ill enough alone.

I lit a match and held it to the end of my pipe until its warm glow cast its spell over Redmoat's ornate dining room. I would have much to discuss with Nayland Smith upon his return from Philadelphia in the morning. Eltham breathed in the fumes from my pipe greedily, like a starving man. His nostrils quivered as the thin layer of flesh around his skull tightened. The veins beneath his widow's peak stood out as if they were lines on a street map until, at once, he relaxed and their color receded into soft pink flesh once more.

"In a way, it could be said that you were the father of my book, Petrie. Had it not been for the success of your Yellow Peril stories, Neville McBride would never have approached me about publishing my memoirs. He certainly could never have persuaded me to document those dark days in China had you not first reminded the world that 'Parson Dan' yet lives and the same shadow from the East that fell upon Western Civilization during the time of the Boxers still poses a threat to the Empire."

He chuckled again as if it were but a fond memory of youthful indiscretions.

"Had I not met McBride, I might never have met Ursula. Without her, I would never have found the strength to walk away from the ministry. I now live a life I once deemed impossible and I owe it all to you, Petrie."

I nodded appreciatively, but truth be told, I was quite uncomfortable having the burden of such a responsibility laid squarely upon my shoulders. Eltham's world had revolved around his faith and his daughter to the exclusion of all else for so long that it seemed strange to hear him speak of anything else. This new woman in his life may have given him the resolve to change horses in midstream, but in so doing, she had also transformed a man I knew and respected into someone that I now barely recognized.

"How is Greba?" I ventured.

Eltham shrugged.

"Fine, I suppose. We're…estranged at the moment, but I trust she'll come round…eventually. She doesn't approve of Ursula…or of the Brotherhood…or of my book, for that matter." He laughed and, for a fleeting moment, I detected that familiar boyish quality behind the lines of his face. "She fears her poor old father is courting disaster."

So Greba didn't approve of the Brotherhood. Difficult as it was to believe, the fact remained that Eltham was now a member of the Brotherhood of Magi. The very concept seemed ludicrous. The devout churchman I knew of old had an intolerance of secret societies that was nearly papist in its intensity. I could not be certain whether he perceived my distaste for this radical change in his thinking or if his mind had wandered elsewhere as he suddenly grew deathly serious.

"I have been alone for so very long, Petrie. Greba has no idea how difficult it has been for me since her mother died."

"You've not been alone, Daniel." It felt strange to call him by his first name when he had always been Reverend Eltham before. "You've had Greba and…"

"I was alone." The words formed a pronouncement, not an opinion. His sudden, piercing stare made me distinctly uncomfortable. "A daughter is poor company for a blind, believing old fool. Empty, Petrie, my life was empty. I have something…substantive now. I have companionship, camaraderie, love, and…and something greater than love."

My face must have betrayed my thoughts.

"You must think me a mad old fool. Well, remember then that madmen accomplish much in this world. I have no regrets if I am counted amongst their number. There were many who thought me mad when I sought to convert the heathen Chinese to Christianity. However, there is a marked difference between the path I was on in those dreary days and the one that I now walk. It is the difference between madness and sanity. The truth is no illusion, Petrie. It cannot be conjured out of nothingness by faith alone."

"Yes, well…" I stood up abruptly. "I've never been much for proselytizing, but I am happy for you if you have truly found what has been missing from your life, Daniel. I only hope you can repair whatever rift exists between you and Greba. It has been nice seeing you again. Truly, it has. Still, I really must be going... the weather outside is simply abominable and I haven't the luxury of sleeping in late in the morning."

J. D. Eltham was a genuine hero who had faithfully served Crown and God in a land hostile to both at the turn of the century, and had gone on to survive two nightmarish encounters in as many years with the terrible aftermath of the Boxer Uprising right here, in the very heart of England itself. He could not have passed through any of these ordeals if a man of formidable strength and character did not lie beneath the guise of the mild-mannered cleric.

At the same time, England might never have learned the name of Dr. Fu Manchu had Eltham not brought his zealous brand of evangelization to China all those years ago. I may have been the father of Eltham's book, but he had summoned that awful specter from the past whose pall would enshroud Britain until the flame of hatred ignited by men like Eltham had finally been extinguished.

I have no recollection of Daniel's expression as I retrieved my hat and coat from the rack in the hall. Quickly donning them, I stepped out into the cold night air with the rain and the snow. As I reached my automobile, I glanced back at Redmoat feeling I might never see her great halls again when my eye caught a light from a tower window in the West Wing. A woman appeared to be standing there as if she were deliberately watching me.

For half a moment, I thought it must be Greba, but I knew it could not be Eltham's daughter who stood there observing my departure. The mysterious figure held a flickering candle in her right hand and appeared to be making some sort of queer gesture with her left. No sooner had this wondrous apparition appeared than she vanished from view as if she had been nothing more than an image of the distant past resurrected for some dark and sinister purpose. Little wonder I could think of nothing else save that bewitching figure on the long road home.

## 3. OF ARMS AND MEN I SING

"No!"

I was panting and covered in sweat. I could recall nothing of the dream, but I knew instinctively that I was safe in my bed once more. My troubling dinner at Redmoat now seemed a lifetime ago.

For half a second, I wondered whether I had indeed shouted aloud or only imagined it. I listened for the sound of Smith's door opening and the inevitable pad of his footsteps as he would cross the hall in but a few short strides and burst through my bedroom door. There was no sound of him stirring. I remembered then he would not return from his trip to Philadelphia until morning. There was so much I was eager to tell him once we met for breakfast at the Fox and Anchor.

Nayland Smith was the finest man I knew. We had been friends since childhood and either of us would have gladly laid down our life to save the other. How many times had he momentarily paused just inside my doorway listening for telltale signs as I imagined him doing just now? The same survival skills that kept him alive during the years he spent stationed in the primitive jungles of Burma had been put to use in our civilized London apartment to quickly ascertain my well-being on numerous occasions.

"It's alright, Smith. It was just a dream."

I would speak in the darkness. He would sigh and I would just be able to make out his hand running through his hair in frustration as he stepped out of the faintly-lit doorway and into the darkness of my room. I would feel him sit at the edge of the bed.

"Was it another dream about Kara?" He would ask.

I would nod, even though there was no way he could see me.

The sound of a striking match would bring a glimmer of light to the room. Nayland's eyes always looked sharp and white...like a tiger's...as he sat on the bed, watching me. The familiar aroma of his tobacco would fill my lungs as he slowly puffed at his pipe until its burning embers would light up his face in shards of red and gold. Nayland's unblinking gaze would penetrate me, violating every place I felt secure. There had been no hiding anything from him when we were boys; it was no different now that we were men.

"I never dream of Kara. I only wish I did. I used to dream of her constantly, but I haven't in weeks, I swear it. I don't know why. I ...I worry for her every waking moment, but when I sleep, it...it is the face of Fu Manchu that fills my thoughts."

I imagined Smith staring at me in the weird light of his pipe.

"You need rest, Petrie. Forget about chasing ghosts. Go back to sleep."

For all I knew, he was right. Kara might be nothing more than a ghost whilst I was still cursed to walk among the living. Smith vanished in a billowing cloud of my own pipe smoke as I lay back on my pillow and began reciting Virgil's *Arma Virumque Cano* until sleep claimed me once more.

The windowpane squeaked beneath my fist as I cleared a small peephole giving me my first look at the world this morning. Winter had descended on London.

Bundled forms could be seen darting from building to building, seeking shelter from the bitterly cold wind. A sputtering cab struggled to navigate the icy street below without colliding into one of the many automobiles that clogged Fleet Street.

I turned from the frost-covered window and sat before the fire. It seemed so terribly distant and unreal, but it had been less than three years since Nayland Smith returned from Burma that summer day in 1911 and sought my aid in his battle against the deadly criminal organization, the Si-Fan and the sinister genius of their chief operative, a man known only by the unlikely moniker of Dr. Fu Manchu.

The Si-Fan was the most dangerous of the many criminal societies that plagued our world. Far more than a mere tong, the membership of the Si-Fan comprised not only Chinese, but also Japanese, Arab, Jew, Egyptian, African, Greeks, European, even Englishmen. The foulest criminal born of the lower classes and the most respectable professional produced by the upper classes of these many great nations had banded together for the single purpose of driving the West from the East and hastening the decline of the British Empire.

The diabolical genius and daring cunning of Dr. Fu Manchu was the Si-Fan*'s* great hope in achieving this purpose. The tenacity and resourcefulness of one solitary Burmese Police Commissioner who had stumbled across Dr. Fu Manchu's path, and subsequently alerted the governments of the West of the threat posed by this most secret of all societies, was our only hope for survival against the superior intellect that guided the Si-Fan.

The task before him was a daunting one. Nayland Smith realized that, if he was to survive this war against an enemy who lurked in the shadows, then he would have to rely on more than just police protection. I became, upon request, his bodyguard and near-constant companion. My decision to stand by my oldest friend in his time of need had an additional benefit in giving me the opportunity to finally put pen to paper, and allowed a simple doctor to realize a long-held dream of becoming an author. More importantly, my renewed association with Smith had the unintended benefit of introducing me to the only woman I have ever truly loved.

She was called Karamaneh. The strange name given her by the cruel desert slave traders who sold her to the Si-Fan when she was but a child was the only one she knew. To me, it would always evoke images of the most radiant jewel of the East. From the first instant I laid eyes upon her, my very soul had belonged to that mysterious, dark-eyed girl. Kara had saved Smith and my life on more than one occasion when we had fallen into the Devil Doctor's clutches.

As I sat before the fire, my thoughts filled with the image of her full, red lips; the deep ocean of her dark, blazing eyes; and the soft tinkle of her lyrical, innocent laughter. I winced at the thought of all that her captivity entailed. The barbaric punishment she must have suffered at the cruel hand of Fu Manchu filled me with rage. But perhaps even more, I feared to think what terrible deeds she was being made to perform. How many men had she bedeviled with her kisses? How many passionate caresses had doomed an unwitting lover to a life of slavery or death? I shook my head to clear my mind of such torturous ruminations, consoling myself in the knowledge that she had given her heart to no man, save me.

Perhaps I was a fool, dreaming I could ever find happiness with a devout Muslim. Even if she were one day freed of the taint of Fu Manchu, where would we find the commonality with which to build a life together? Until I entered her world, the only solace she had found was in the love of her brother, Aziz. A gentle if sickly youth, the boy shared his sister's delicate beauty. He was the only family Kara had left since their older sister died whilst the three of them crossed the Egyptian desert as children in a caravan of slave traders. I shall never comprehend how two such sensitive creatures ever survived a life in which affection and discipline were meted out equally with cruel lashes from the slaver's whip.

What of me? What could I offer her apart from my heart? What did I even know of love save the intensely burning passion that overtook me the very instant I first laid eyes upon her soft and dusky face? What could the only child of a loveless marriage know of making a woman happy? My father, for all of his brilliance, cared for naught but unearthing the forgotten treasures of the past. His legacy to me was an appreciation of foreign cultures and a crippling inability to forge lasting relationships. If not for Nayland…noble, courageous Nayland, I would truly have been alone in the world.

Now the days seemed long, it had been several weeks since there had been any trace of Si-Fan activity in London. I feared that Fu Manchu and company had returned to China, taking Kara along with them. It was just a question of time before this prolonged inactivity resulted in Nayland being recalled to his post in Burma. I looked around the silent, cluttered rooms Smith leased from his friend, Colonel Bickerstaff. It was impossible to feel at ease among the grotesque Indian curios that adorned every table and shelf. The apartment offered little in the way of comfort, but then no lodging could mend a life irreparably broken under the hand of Fu Manchu.

I glanced up at the massive wooden frame of the stern-faced grandfather clock that dominated the far corner of the study and swept the few pages I had managed to produce last night into a pile. I placed them out of our housekeeper's reach by concealing them in a hollowed-out copy of the King James Bible that I had inherited from my father. Best use yet found for the Word of God, he used to say. Sometimes I wondered if he regretted such remarks after he died, or if that magnificent mind of his had ceased to crackle with activity at the same moment his eyes lost their light.

That was the root of religious belief, I mused, the fear that death is actually a bridge rather than the finale of life's symphony. I replaced the book in the snug gap in the top row of the towering bookshelf. I cursed myself for my procrastination. There was no time now for a cup of tea and I would surely regret its absence later. I hurried to meet Nayland Smith for breakfast as we had agreed we would do upon his return from the States. Happily, the season guaranteed that cabs were still plentiful on Fleet Street despite the inclement weather.

A little over an hour later, I stood outside the Fox and Anchor, a solitary snow-covered figure among the ever-moving throng of shoppers and merry-makers who bustled up and down the crowded street this morning. It was strange to think that London was ready to embrace still another Christmas in blissful ignorance of the ever-present threat of some new outrage. My thoughts turned back to Eltham. He had rung me up to ask me over for dinner. Such an occurrence was not exceptional, as Eltham and I had always got on well and it had been far too long since we had seen one another. It had come as quite a shock to learn all the changes his life had seen in the months since Smith and I had saved him from the torture of the wire jacket.

As the minutes ticked by, I began to grow restless, watching my exhaled breath cloud the cold morning air. I cast a quick glance over my shoulder in the direction of my departed cab. When I turned back, I saw a taxi, tarnished with slush and snow, pull up to the curb and deposit Nayland Smith only a few yards from where I stood.

Smith was as unchanging as the sun. He was the fixed point against which the rest of the world could set its compass. The hawk-like nose and jutting chin made his profile ripe for caricature. He had a face that was never young and yet, a single one of his rare smiles would roll back the years. The creases that had been prematurely carved around his tiny mouth would disappear leaving only the touch of grey around his temples to mar that otherwise flawless portrait of British virility.

"You're more than a bit under-dressed." I chuckled in response to the absence of muffler and gloves. "How was the voyage over?"

Smoke-colored eyes disappeared in the crevices of that cherished smile as he grasped my outstretched hand in a firm, but decidedly frozen greeting. His features, perennially suntanned from years of being stationed in Burma, made him stand out even more among his fellow Londoners.

"My visit and passage were both mercifully uneventful, but let's save the pleasantries until we're safely indoors, Petrie."

He pointed in the direction of the inviting pub with a manila folder clasped firmly in his left hand. The Fox and Anchor was bustling despite the weather. Nothing short of a blizzard would keep its regular clientele away and Smith and I were certainly no exception. Once we were seated inside, and Smith had barked our order to the waiter, he set the manila folder down on the table and began fussing with his pipe.

"Enjoyed the time off, I trust?" he asked, but didn't wait for my response. "Checked to see how Dr. Murray is faring with your old practice, I'd imagine. No better than you would be, I'm sure. My visit was certainly no match for a picnic on Gezirah Island, I can tell you." He tugged at his left earlobe in annoyance. "I had a bit of business to mull over while I was in Philadelphia looking in on my late brother's family."

"Oh?"

He shook his head. "Ah, good, here's our breakfast, then."

I knew there was no pressuring Smith. It was best to just share his distractions. Such interruptions were necessary for him to maintain the frenetic pace he adopted when activity was demanded. Besides, I had sorely missed the Fox and Anchor's smoked salmon, scrambled eggs, steak and kidney pie while I was in Cairo. Happily, it had become my staple breakfast again since Smith had dragged me back into this Si-Fan business.

The waiter set our plates before us and we spent the next few minutes enjoying our meal in silence. We were seated at a small table adjacent to the large front window. From the warmth of the restaurant, our view of the falling snow resembled a picture postcard come to life. Neither of us possessed an aptitude for trivial conversation, but we shared the same values and that made it unnecessary to reinforce our friendship with idle chatter.

"No," Smith began speaking as if no time had elapsed in our conversation. "I also had to look over part of a manuscript from a...a small publishing house here in

London…McBride & Valley. Certainly not my usual sort of assignment, but there was good reason for the request."

"Yes, I think I can guess…"

"It seems our old friend, Eltham…"

"I know all about it, Smith."

"…has decided to write a book. Damn fool idea if you ask me, but he didn't, regrettably."

"Smith, I said I know."

"Now be patient a moment and I'll explain. Eltham intends to tell all that happened to him during the Boxer Uprising. Here, it's worth having a look."

He began sorting through the pages in the manila folder.

"Smith, did you hear what I said?"

"What? Oh, of course I heard you…every word. Now here, have a look, won't take a moment."

I took the pages from him as my eyes scanned their content.

*How much time elapsed, I had no way of knowing. My first recollection was of a warm wetness on my brow and of a gentle hand stroking my cheek. I thought of Freda for a fleeting second. My eyes opened and I struggled to adjust to the blinding whiteness that enveloped me. I thought I had died and awoken in Paradise as I beheld the most beautiful face I have ever seen.*

*I tore the wet cloth from my forehead as I bolted upright in my bed. The woman smiled and gently pushed me back down and pulled the sheet up around my heaving chest. I felt myself melting as I disappeared inside those gorgeous walnut-colored eyes. Naked desire overwhelmed my senses. I would have given my soul to crush that tall, graceful figure in my arms and smother those perfect lips with burning kisses.*

*She spoke and brought me out of my fantasy. Her voice was lower than I expected. I gradually identified the dialect she spoke as Russian or some similar barbaric tongue. She smiled at my lack of comprehension and repeated her words in slow, deliberate English. I nodded that I understood this time. She told me that I was in the Christian hospital at Nan-King where I would be safe.*

*My eyes travelled around the sparsely decorated room until they settled on a beautiful painting of Saint Joseph somberly looking down upon the weeping form of the boy Savior that he held cradled in his arms. The portrait's faded colors had bled together until they resembled a dull monochrome. It was no small comfort to be back among civilized men at last.*

*She asked where I came from and I explained that I was one of the English missionaries that had chosen to remain behind. I was the only survivor now. The Boxers had seen to that. She nodded sadly and said the doctor would be in to see me soon. Later perhaps I would dine with the head of their mission. I watched her closely as she spoke. The subtle changes in her face and tone made it obvious her feelings for this man ran deep.*

*The door on the opposite side of the room opened and an old man dressed in the garb of a doctor entered with the support of a cane. The lovely young nurse whose name I still did not know rose and quickly crossed to his side, taking his arm and helping him over to my bed with great care. They conversed about me in German with only a few fleeting glances in my direction as if I were an animal and not a man. The old man grunted the odd response and nodded curtly to her as she spoke. I watched longingly as she left the room without as much as a glance back in my direction.*

*The old man bent over me and began his examination. A thumb and forefinger roughly pulled back my eyelids one at a time. I struggled to look at the ceiling, but I could not break from his gaze. I had never beheld such magnetic eyes. They were a true cat-green and shone with an unnatural intelligence. As I gazed up into them, a thin filmy membrane appeared to cloud over his pupils. I felt a force sear through my brain as he stared down at me. His lined face betrayed not a glimmer of emotion as I studied each of the crevices that burrowed deep down into the flesh of his cheeks and forehead. My gaze travelled up to study the thin outline of white hair that covered his large, protruding skull.*

"I am Doktor Schmidt, Herr Eltham. Guten tag."

*His halting English came in a rough, hoarse rasp with a peculiar emphasis on the wrong syllables as if he had learnt the language without ever having heard it spoken by a native.*

"I am here to help you."

*He reached a long, skeletal hand out to grasp mine. I recoiled in disgust. His smile twisted into a grisly grimace as the effeminate thin blue lips that formed a ring about his cruel mouth were stretched taut.*

"Do you find it difficult placing your life in the hands of a German doctor? Even one who studied at Heidelberg? Perhaps you would find it comforting to know I answered to an Anglo-Saxon name when I was at Edinburgh or a French name when I was at the Sorbonne. Identities are meaningless to one who has...alas, I fear my attempt to reason with you have only sown the seeds of confusion. Your feeble English mind cannot begin to comprehend that which your very eyes now perceive."

*As he spoke, his features began to yellow like the pages of some ancient text or as if he was suddenly stricken with some rapidly progressing jaundice.*

*"You English fancy yourself superior to these peoples of China because they herald not from your Christian West."*

*His eyes burned into mine with a fervor that was impossible to resist.*

*"You forget that the blood which stains your hands is not of beasts, but of men."*

*I looked at my hands and saw the spreading stain. In my heart, I knew he was right. No matter how hard I tried, I would never be clean again.*

"Good Heavens!" My fork clattered loudly as it hit my plate. "Smith, do you realize what this means?"

Smith flashed a grim smile and nodded his head.

"We finally have confirmation of what we have long suspected, Petrie. Eltham met the man we know as Dr. Fu Manchu whilst he was in China at the turn of the century. Fu Manchu was posing as a German doctor... doubtless to undermine the work of Western missionaries. The only reason Eltham is alive today is because he has not set eyes on Fu Manchu since that time, and is unaware that the Chinaman who imperiled his life twice in the past two years and the German doctor he met in the missionary are one and the same. This book of Eltham's may unwittingly expose Dr. Fu Manchu's real identity to members of the Chinese government with enough integrity and clout to take action against him, as they have so often sworn to do in the past. The Si-Fan is placed in dire straits for perhaps the first time in their infamous history.

"The Home Office got wind of Eltham's memoirs and asked me to look over the manuscript whilst I was in

Philadelphia. Unfortunately, the publisher only provided a few brief excerpts and nothing more. It is imperative that we speak with Eltham as soon as possible and halt publication of this foolhardy book of his before it is too late. His very life may depend upon our success."

"But, Smith," I cried. "That's just what I've been trying to tell you. I dined with Eltham at Redmoat only last night. He was celebrating the completion of his manuscript. His book is ready for publication and he's positively elated at the prospect of revealing his role in stirring up the Boxer Uprising to the rest of the world."

"Great Scott! If word of his memoirs has spread, it is likely he is already being watched by the Si-Fan. If you were observed visiting Redmoat, then we may already be too late! Finish your glass. We leave immediately."

## 4. ILL FORTUNE

It had been more than two years since Nayland Smith had last set foot on the grounds of Redmoat. The ancient priory originally christened "Round Moat" during the reign of Henry VIII in 1536 still stood, like so much of our island nation, as a reminder of our past glories. Redmoat remained surrounded by shrubbery and elms on all sides. The maze of shrubs parted in the center and led to the banks of the Waverney.

There was an air of tranquility about the place which instilled in me the conviction that a rural existence was the one intended for man and that we had failed in seeking civilization in our stone and brick cells. The moat which gave the estate its name still exists, although it is no longer flooded, and is used as nothing more than a cabbage garden. The barbed wire fencing and complex electrical alarm system whose wires wound along the perimeter of the moat were proof that Eltham also appreciated its strategic value.

Redmoat rests on an artificial mound, the half-obscured ruins of one of Hadrian's outposts. As the moat is no longer the principle means of isolation, the narrow tributary of the Waverney to the East and the High Road which runs nearly twenty feet below the perpendicular banks to the North and the West serve the same purpose. Entrance to this remarkable fortress is afforded via a heavy iron gate admissible only through a break in the encircling shrubbery.

These very precautions were foremost in my mind as we reached the opening in the shrubbery to discover an unlocked gate before us. We said nothing, but I knew Smith was as apprehensive as I that this breach in security was a harbinger of ill fortune.

We trudged our way up the hillside path past the snow-covered hedges and trees that protected Eltham's privacy from the outside world until we found ourselves facing a towering snowman standing guard at the top of the ridge like a giant sentinel stationed before the house.

I gasped at the sight of it, but quickly found myself chuckling at the thought of children succeeding in startling, with very little effort, a grown man who has seen his fair share of genuine terrors.

As I made my way up the path to the front steps, I turned to see what was keeping Smith. To my surprise, he had wandered off the path and was carefully observing the snowman. He never partook in such pursuits when we were schoolboys ourselves. Consequently, I was quite puzzled to find him so easily distracted now by something so mundane.

"What seems to be the trouble?" I asked.

"It's so lifelike," he mumbled, staring into the face of the snowman.

"That is the general idea," I said as I knocked upon the thick wooden door.

I waited patiently for a moment, only vaguely aware that Smith was still preoccupied. There was no response. Irritated, I knocked a second time with considerably greater force.

"Petrie," Smith's voice sounded oddly hollow. "I wouldn't worry too much about trying to rouse someone now. Whatever you do, it won't be enough to raise Eltham."

I turned to see what the Devil he was on about when I noticed Smith's attention was still directed to the snowman we had passed on our way up the path. Without a word, Smith stepped forward and toppled the snowman over onto its back.

Frostbitten, discolored flesh now protruded from various spots on the snow-covered form. Gradually, I recognized the various bits of flesh as belonging to a cheekbone, forearm, abdomen, thigh, and leg. My head swam at the sight before us. The grayish tinge of pulpy flesh contrasted sharply with the terrible deathly whiteness of the snow.

"It's Eltham, Petrie. He's dead."

Smith's voice chilled me to the bone. I felt nauseous.

As a medical man, I was accustomed to seeing death in all its many forms. At this moment, I knew I had never witnessed a sight as ghastly as the discovery of our old friend, unclothed and dead, concealed within the form of a snowman in the heart of Surrey barely four weeks before Christmas.

## 5. THE PARSON'S WHORE

"This gruesome murder can only be the work of Dr. Fu Manchu," I said as I stared out of the window at the snow-covered mound where Eltham had met his hideous and ignominious death.

Nayland Smith nodded grimly as he entered the room behind me.

"I've just telephoned Inspector Weymouth. He'll be here as soon as he can. I have asked him to be discreet. There is nothing to be gained from alerting the local authorities and causing a public uproar if one can be avoided."

Inspector John Weymouth was the CID man assigned to the Fu Manchu case. He was big enough a man to recognize that. although only a colonial administrator, Nayland Smith, by virtue of his past experience with the Si-Fan, was more of an expert in the dealings of these cunning devils than Weymouth could ever hope to be.

Smith tugged at his left earlobe in irritation as he began to pace about the room with his hands locked behind his back.

"So Eltham had turned his back on the Church and embraced Theosophy, had he?" Smith rubbed his chin as he ruminated.

"So it would seem. He also lost his daughter in the process. I don't think Greba approved of the company he had been keeping."

Smith's smoldering grey eyes twinkled in the light from the fireplace. "Wouldn't wonder at that, Petrie…wouldn't wonder at all. Still, Eltham was never really respectable in the sense that most churchmen are…"

He trailed off in mid-thought as he often did when his mind was racing to consider the best possible course of action. "Tell me what you learned of this book of his," Smith snapped.

"Well, I'm sure there's very little I can add that you haven't already gleaned. The title of the manuscript is *Man o' God*. The publication date has not yet been set. In fact, from Eltham's remarks as well as yours I gather this McBride & Valley is very much a small-scale publishing venture."

I broke off as I was struck by a sudden thought.

"It certainly is remarkable that Eltham would even consider addressing all that transpired during his years in China. He was always loath to discuss anything to do with the Boxers, even when he and Greba were personally imperiled by the Si-Fan…"

"Petrie," Smith came to a sudden halt as he interrupted me. "What did you say was the name of that woman Eltham had mentioned?"

I stammered for a moment trying to recollect the name.

Smith snapped his fingers three times as if it would help jar my failing memory.

"It wasn't Ursula, was it?"

"Why, yes, I believe it was."

"Last name?" Smith snapped.

"I…I don't recall."

"Don't recall or never told?"

"No, I'm quite sure that he referred to her by her first name only."

"You're positive that it was Ursula?"

Smith's dogged perseverance in the face of obscure details was often difficult to bear.

"I'm almost certain that it was. What significance do you attach to the name?"

Smith paced for a moment before turning to face me once more.

"I would hazard a guess that the lady in question is called Ursula Trelawney."

He spoke the name deliberately as if it should convey some special meaning.

"Who the Devil is Ursula Trelawney?"

He took his pipe from his breast pocket and gestured with it.

"Ursula Trelawney is the first woman to be admitted to the ranks of the Brotherhood of Magi. She was born in 1891 on the same day and, in fact, mere minutes after the recorded death of Madame Blavatsky, the self-proclaimed Priestess of Isis and founder of Theosophy. This seemingly insignificant coincidence, and the young lady's accomplishments in the Black Arts in such few short years, have convinced a number of interested parties that she is none other than the reincarnation of that infamous woman herself."

I cleared my throat awkwardly.

"I don't wish to be droll, Smith, but you know I put as much stock in reincarnation as I do in transubstantiation. I fail to see why any of this is of the slightest significance if it doesn't lead us to apprehending Dr. Fu Manchu."

Smith murmured as he lit his pipe, "It may do just that, Petrie. It may do just that."

I waited impatiently while he puffed away at the pipe until he was ready to continue.

"Mistress Trelawney's reputation extends well beyond mere conjuring tricks like sleight of hand or conversing with the dead by means of séance. No, the young lady has instead established a name for herself in allegedly succeeding in realizing the dream of many an alchemist of old."

"Which particular dream would that be?" I asked.

"I speak of the extension of human life. She claims to have perfected the means of holding off death and extending life…possibly without limit."

I laughed at the very suggestion of such simple-minded rot.

"That is certainly an intriguing area of study for a young lady of barely 20. Does this entail her bathing in yak's milk or in the blood of freshly-murdered virgins?"

"I have no idea," Smith said, "but I can assure you that a man of Dr. Fu Manchu's advanced age, fragile health, and undeniable genius would certainly find merit in her research. What is more, we have Eltham's own word that it was the Brotherhood of Magi who convinced him to disclose all he said, did, and heard at the time of the Boxers. If there was any question whether these facts have escaped Fu Manchu's notice, one need only consider Eltham's fate."

"Then Ursula Trelawney's life is in jeopardy as well?"

"I have made no such statement, Petrie. I have merely noted that the thread which sews together the lives of those involved with Eltham may equally bind them to the Si-Fan. There is little to be gained if we act with haste. When human lives are hanging in the balance, we cannot carelessly play the heroes' part as if this were just some sort of melodramatic thriller."

My heart sank. My eagerness to please was proof of my unsuitability to the task at hand. My father had said as much to me on his deathbed. I couldn't bear disappointing Nayland as well.

"Don't be so hard on yourself, Petrie. You mean well and I know it, but your heart rules your head, as always. You never cease hoping we uncover some clue that somehow points back to Kara and allows us to win her freedom. This is a hard road we have chosen. If you are to walk it with me, then you must forget that girl and keep your wits about you. I don't mean to say that all is lost, but you must let your memories sleep in your mind. Love is the way of misery and has been man's undoing since woman first offered him a taste of her forbidden fruit in the Garden of Delights. It will always be this way. You must learn this lesson for yourself before it costs you your life…or mine."

Smith turned away from me and resumed his interminable pacing when without warning he came to an abrupt stop just as suddenly as he had started.

"We know that someone had obviously paid a visit to Eltham here last night after your departure and they didn't go to the trouble of locking the doors behind them when they left. Bad luck that he had dismissed Edwards and the rest of the staff. Even more so that he got rid of those mastiffs of his. They certainly would have been welcome last night."

We passed through the Old World dining room and into the library. Feeling overwhelmed by all that had happened since my dinner with Eltham, I sat in the chair next to the big wooden table with the shaded lamp and stared at the mantelpiece opposite with its dimly-illuminated candles in their ancient sconces.

This place seemed so empty without the Eltham of old: perennially nervous, brisk, boyish, acutely sensitive, a peculiar mix of pride and remorse for his storied past. He was not the same man without Greba by his side. She was the perfect daughter for a lonely old man. An uncommonly fetching girl; wide-eyed and tanned skinned and as clever a beast as one could hope to find. It was difficult to believe that anyone or anything could have come between a father and daughter with so close a bond.

Smith had busied himself nosing among the rows of towering bookshelves that covered each wall of the room.

"Petrie," he asked, "you weren't, by chance, in this room yesterday evening?"

"No. Why do you ask?"

Smith paused for a moment while handling a book. His eyes scanned the pages quickly as if he were seeking a particular word. His intense concentration and his beak-like nose leant him the appearance of a bird of prey. He replaced the book on the shelf and turned to face me.

"I ask because I am curious about the change in this library since I was last at Redmoat."

I shook my head in astonishment.

"Smith, how can you possibly notice such a trivial detail as a change in a library you have not set foot in for nearly three years? That memory of yours sometimes unsettles me."

"Thank you, but I don't pretend to recall the slightest detail of this library from our previous visit. It is the absence of the sort of books that one would expect to find in a churchman's library and the inclusion of just the sort of titles that one would not expect that tells me the contents of this room have changed dramatically."

I rose from my seat and crossed the room to stand by his side. The bookcase on my immediate left was filled with almanacs, travel guides, encyclopedias, and dictionaries. Many titles were of an Oriental character. This was hardly surprising considering Eltham's years of missionary service in that part of the world. However, the bookcase in front of me and indeed the one to its right and, it transpired, every remaining shelf in the library was filled with occult tomes.

"Where are his Bibles…his Concordances…his Lectionaries?" Smith asked as he gestured around the room. "Where are the writings of the Early Church Fathers?"

Smith was correct, not a trace remained of his earlier life. It was as if Eltham desired a clean break with the past and any reminder of who he once was had been too painful to bear.

"Perhaps the books are in storage somewhere with Greba or with Vernon?" I said in reference to Eltham's nephew who had lived with him and his daughter at the time we first made their acquaintance.

Smith shook his head. "Not very likely, I'm afraid. My guess would be that he burned them. He wanted no memory of Christianity in this home. It wouldn't have sat well with his new…er, interests." Smith gestured toward the shelves in front of us.

"That's not necessarily the case, Smith. Even during his missionary days, books concerning occult practices and activities might have had a place in his library. One must know one's enemy before one can hope to defeat him."

"You're not thinking clearly, Petrie," Smith snapped. "Eltham had no time for the beliefs of others. His approach to evangelization was to grind every last vestige of Paganism into dust. No, what you see around us came about once that Trelawney woman got her clutches into him. The Eltham we knew would have sooner died than seen Redmoat littered with this diabolic filth."

"Speaking of filth," I said as I ran a finger along the bookshelf. "It is obvious that this house has not been kept up since the servants were dismissed."

"No, nor are there any photographs of Greba...or her mother. That is something I distinctly recall seeing before," Smith said as he eyed the room distastefully.

I recalled the framed photographs of Freda Eltham that had adorned nearly every room of the house. I felt ashamed that I had not noticed their absence when I was here the night before. Greba bore such a strong resemblance to her mother. She must have been quite young when she was killed by the Boxers. The poor child had known so much tragedy in her short life and now her Christmases would be tainted evermore once she learned of her father's murder.

A creaking floorboard startled me out of my reverie. Smith grasped my arm tightly. Someone else was in the house and, judging by the sound, almost directly above us on the second floor. We drew our revolvers and dashed out into the hallway.

My senses were alert for the slightest indication of movement. Eltham's assassin was still here in Redmoat right along with us. Dr. Fu Manchu counted dacoits, phansigars, and thuggees among his followers. Each encounter with the Si-Fan was a dance with death and we both knew a single misstep would cost us our lives. Like men possessed, we dashed up the staircase to the second floor. Before we had even reached the landing, my heart missed a beat as we were greeted by the most unexpected sight imaginable.

Standing at the top of the stairs was a staggeringly beautiful woman, completely nude but for the towel which barely concealed her modesty. Water dripped from every inch of her perfect form. The towel slipped provocatively as she placed both hands on her hips.

"There is little need for heroics, gentlemen." She nodded toward our revolvers. "I assure you I am unarmed."

"What...what are you doing here?" I stammered in complete befuddlement.

She was a splendidly fantastic creature with a proud, haughty mouth; blazing, imperious eyes; and an unruly mane of thick, wet brown hair that cascaded down around her smooth ivory shoulders. Most staggering of all was the fact that she appeared completely at ease standing before two strange men in a state of undress.

"That is a question I might very well ask the both of you," she said as she adjusted the towel beneath her arms. "I live here. What business do you have? Are you friends of Daniel's?"

Her tone had not softened whilst her eyes searched ours questioningly. It was evident that she had no clue as to the awful fate that had befallen Eltham.

"Yes, we are," I replied. "I am Dr. Petrie and this is Police Commissioner Denis Nayland Smith of Burma."

I stepped up to the landing and extended my card. She let the towel drop to one side as she accepted it.

"You must forgive my poor manners, gentlemen. I am Ursula Trelawney. I am a clairvoyant by trade and some of my clients prefer I make house calls. I'm sure you understand, Doctor." Her voice tinkled like a stone skipping across glass. She appeared to find humor in her lack of propriety. "Daniel prefers that I extend my visit to multiple days...and nights. I must say how refreshing it is to find gentlemen that are worldly enough not to behave as though they find my presence here at Redmoat to be scandalous in any fashion. Mankind's progress has been stymied for far too many centuries by spineless little men with the petty morals of tired old spinsters."

"I thought you might be turning up before long," Nayland Smith murmured as he returned his revolver to its holster and climbed the few remaining steps to join me on the landing. "I fear we bring bad tidings concerning your friend, Daniel. He's dead."

For a second, Ursula Trelawney's eyes searched Smith's in concern, but the appearance of emotion was fleeting.

"Is he? I wondered where he'd got to."

Smith clicked his tongue in mock reproach.

"I would have expected a clairvoyant to be able to foresee a tragedy of such magnitude befalling one of her regular clients...particularly one willing to pay for lengthy visits to allow for more accurate readings. I do hope this isn't a blemish on your reputation."

The blazing imperiousness returned to her eyes.

"Have a care, Mr. Smith." Her voice was like frozen rain dropping against a window. "A gentleman is expected to show common courtesy to a lady when delivering such tragic news."

"Oh, come now, Miss Trelawney..." Smith chuckled. "I am no more a gentleman than you are a..."

The woman gasped in astonishment.

Smith feigned concern at her response.

"Did I offend you just now?" he asked with faux sincerity. "Forgive me, Miss Trelawney, I wouldn't have expected a parson's whore to possess such delicate sensibilities."

"I am no man's whore," Ursula Trelawney replied with a shrug of her shoulders. "I love whomever I please."

"Love must be the most abused word in the English language," Smith spat contemptuously.

She stretched her arms above her head as she tried to stifle a yawn and allowed the towel to fall to her feet. The brazen, shameless creature shook her head faintly as if to remove any excess water and ran a hand through her tousled hair.

"I would imagine you know all about abuse, Mr. Smith...particularly self-abuse." She took a deep breath and sighed contentedly. "You positively reek of it."

Smith squared his jaw and silently stepped forward and struck her hard across the mouth. She kept her composure admirably, displaying no indication that the blow had inflicted any pain. She smiled at us in perverse delight as she lapped at the trickle of blood welling at the corner of her mouth with a delicate, pink tongue. Dark eyes closed in seeming pleasure as if she savored its very taste.

"Thank you, Mr. Smith." Her voice was a barely audible whisper. "Strike me again. I'm begging for it."

Smith lifted his hand to oblige her when I stepped between them and roughly pushed him back toward the stairs.

"Get a grip on yourself, man! I will not tolerate the mistreatment of a lady."

"Don't be a fool, Petrie..."

Smith's voice trailed off as utter dismay registered on his tanned features.

I turned to see what the matter was when I found to my shock that Ursula Trelawney had seemingly vanished into thin air leaving only a wet towel behind on the floor as proof she was not some phantom born of my overheated imagination.

"Where the Devil did she get to?" I said as Smith pushed past me in a huff.

The silent doorway in front of which she had stood provided the obvious solution to the puzzle. I followed Smith through the unlocked door and discovered myself not in a conventional bathroom as I expected to find from her state of undress, but rather found that we had stumbled into a dimly-lit antechamber of the sort that one finds in H. Bedford-Jones' more fanciful yarns.

A pungent aroma filled the air. I immediately recalled our visit to Shen-Yan's opium den in Limehouse. The room was filled with jade dragons resting upon marble pillars as far as the eye could see. The intoxicating smell of burning opiates wafted from the gaping maws of the many stone dragons that crowded the room. It was difficult to believe that we were still in Redmoat and had not been spirited away, by some inexplicable means, to the Orient.

"Saints preserve us!" Smith gasped.

I looked forward past where he stood and saw a narrow path leading to the end of the room. There, I saw Ursula Trelawney, still nude, stretched out languidly on a divan as if lost in unholy meditation. A powerful, irresistible force compelled us forward. We advanced in single-file formation down the narrow avenue past the smoking jade dragons that lined either side of our path.

I struggled to keep my mind clear as the air was heavy with the intoxicating aroma of the opiate. Past experience had taught me the dreamscapes it conjured could easily far exceed anything de Quincey had recorded for posterity. I noticed the dragons' eyes were set with rubies that sparkled in the suffocating blackness of the room. The same fantastic iridescence produced by the gemstones shone from Ursula Trelawney's eyes and navel as we approached like a pair of devout pilgrims come to worship her burnished flesh. So mesmerized was I by the spectacle of this phantasmagorical sight, that I did not question how a woman's eyes could burn with such supernatural brightness. It was only when we were but a few short steps away from the divan that I realized that we were not gazing upon the magnificent woman who stood before us in the hallway, but rather, her alabaster likeness!

Had the statue been sculpted by Michelangelo himself, it could not have been a more lifelike representation of that fantastic form. I followed Smith's example and lifted a hand to my eyes to shield them from the dazzling pinpoints of light in the darkened, smoke-filled haze. I counted them to be sure that I had not been deceived. Where before there had been only three pinpoints emanating from the statue's eyes and navel, there were now five points of ruby-red lights shining out in the darkness, blinding us.

The other two lights danced and bobbed hypnotically just below her navel. Improper as it may sound, we crouched as we reached the edge of the divan to examine them more closely. A tongue flicked in the darkness just below the shimmering pinpoints of light. I was sure it was the same lascivious tongue I had glimpsed lapping up her own blood after Smith had struck the woman across the mouth. My head was slowly bobbing as I struggled to follow the dancing ruby-red lights. I felt myself struggling to resist the call of sleep and knew that I had fallen completely under their spell.

"Run, Petrie, run! For God's sake, save yourself!"

Smith's voice cried out in the darkness.

I struggled to focus on the sound of his voice and break away from those seductively, hypnotic beacons of light. It was then I saw my old friend writhing in pain. He was bound by some queer jade rope coiled taut about his body. I watched dumbstruck as he was lashed about the room as if he were naught but a rag doll.

I did not want to think about Smith and the strange, inexplicable fate that had befallen him. I turned my eyes back to those dazzling pinpoints of light. I wanted so very much to be lost in their burning brightness once more, but they had vanished. In the moment I had turned aside, the spell had been broken. In their place, I found myself facing that which had bound Smith and was squeezing the life from his helpless form. There in front of me, with eyes shining brightly, obscene tongue flicking putrid, hot breath in my face was the head of the largest serpent I had ever seen in my life.

## 6. SULPHUR AND MERCURY

My heart was pounding furiously. Death was upon us both and there was nothing Nayland Smith or I could do to avoid it. This was no opium-fuelled nightmare despite the pungent odor that lay heavy in the air and clung to our clothing. Smith's face was purple. He bit through his lower lip as the coiled serpent crushed him in its terrible embrace. The gigantic head of the creature was as large as a man's torso. I could feel its foul, fetid breath warm against my cheek as it moved in close to strike.

I shut my eyes and tried to pray, but the words failed me. The echoing pulse of my heart was throbbing in my ears. The smell of the opium, the smell of the serpent's breath, and my fear combined to produce a nausea so overpowering that I was unable to resist. I longed for the horrible monstrosity to finish with me quickly for I had no desire to be conscious of soiling myself in the seconds remaining before the most awful death imaginable claimed me.

The pounding in my ears built to a crescendo. A senses-shattering explosion followed. I waited for an awareness of hemorrhaging, but no blood came. I had but a moment to ponder this peculiar fact when I was overwhelmed by an enormous mass. Conflicting sensations of weightlessness and pain overruled my thoughts before all activity abruptly ceased and I knew no more.

My entrance to the netherworld came from a familiar face, but one I swore was still among the living. Inspector

John Weymouth's grim countenance struggled in and out of my hazy view. His brow was furrowed and his lips parted, but I heard nothing until, with a painful pop, air rushed into both of my ear canals and with it came sound…a glorious rush of wind and noise louder than I ever remembered hearing anything ever before.

"For Christ's sake, Petrie, don't just lie there! Get up and let me put this bloody beast down!"

"Weymouth!" I cried. "It really is you!"

I struggled to my feet and slid about on the blackened floor like a child trying to master his ice skates for the first time.

"Of course it's me!" Weymouth barked. "Now get up and help me see if Smith is still alive!"

Smith? What had happened to Smith? My God, the purple face! I recalled everything now. I grasped onto Weymouth's pant leg with both hands and pulled myself across the floor. The Inspector sent me reeling with one mighty kick before falling upon his backside next to me as an awful thud shook the floor.

I sat up and looked at the still form of the enormous serpent. Three bullet holes had pierced the creature's skull in an alignment possible only for a trained marksman.

"You killed it! Weymouth, you really killed it!"

"Of course I killed it!" Weymouth snarled. "Who did you think fired those shots next to your head, your guardian angel? Bloody big snake to find in the middle of an English winter, I'll say."

"I—I didn't hear them…I thought…"

"Never mind what you thought!" Weymouth barked as he helped me back on my feet. "There's Smith to think of."

As we made our way to the opposite end of the room, where the serpent's tail lay taut and unmoving, we passed by the alabaster divan with its likeness of Ursula Trelawney stretched about it in obscene repose.

"There he is!" Weymouth yelled and rushed off to a dark corner of the antechamber.

I stared at the serpent's tail and looked behind us where its head lay unseeing and still. The creature must have been nearly 35 feet in length. I swallowed hard to stop myself from gagging.

"Petrie! Come quickly!"

I rushed to Weymouth's side and saw him crouching beside the crumpled form of Nayland Smith. The man had been twisted in a terrible position and was motionless, but there was life in him yet. He must have been thrown across the room when the serpent lashed its tail about in its death throes. It was only then that I realized the weight I had felt crushing me had been the enormous head and neck of the creature landing upon me as it fell dead with three bullets in its brain courtesy of the Inspector's revolver.

"Don't move him, Weymouth. We don't know the extent of his injuries. We need to get him to hospital and quickly!"

Weymouth nodded his head, eager to do what he could for our mutual friend.

"Is there a telephone somewhere?" he asked, all of the gruffness in his voice having disappeared out of concern for Smith's well-being.

"Yes, downstairs...main room...the table near the fireplace. But be careful, Weymouth. We may not be alone."

He nodded grimly and set off at a trot.

I was beginning to regain my senses. I remembered I was a doctor above all else. I turned to help tend to the man who mattered most to me in the world.

Weymouth returned shortly. We agreed I should remain with Smith while the Inspector conducted a thorough search of Redmoat. There was no sign of anyone, nor did he find any exit from the room Ursula Trelawney had vanished into apart from the doorway Smith and I had entered off of the hall by the stairwell. I had no explanation for how a nude woman could have escaped out into the snow with no doors or windows leading from the room, but it paled in comparison to explaining how a gargantuan serpent and an obscene statue came to reside in a respectable Surrey estate.

Smith had not yet recovered consciousness and I feared my old friend would never be the same man again. Chalmers Cleeve, the local police surgeon, arrived shortly before Smith was taken to hospital by the ambulance Weymouth had summoned. Cleeve and I spoke about Eltham's terrible fate and I confirmed his suspicions that the Si-Fan was behind the former churchman's death. I offered to assist at the inquest, but Cleeve declined. Weymouth had promised to help track Greba down as well as gather whatever information could be found on Ursula Trelawney. I thanked him again for his help as he made his departure from Redmoat.

The approach of Christmas could not have come at a more dire time. The holiday hung over our heads like a funeral pall. After a few hours at the hospital by Smith's side during which he was still delirious, I accepted his doctor's advice that he needed peace and quiet and the time with which to recover. I decided to return home for some much-needed rest. The doctor inquired as to whether I needed a cab, but I declined believing the cold night air and the solitude would do wonders to clear my head. I barely recognized Lowther Arcade and Charing Cross Station as I passed them by, lost in thought.

I was terribly exhausted after our ordeal at Redmoat and slept better that night than I had in many weeks. It seemed that my head had barely touched the pillow before I found myself transported to that futurity where what was and what may yet be co-exist for the weary dreamer. There was a guide on my astral voyage and I quickly recognized it to be the Egyptian goddess Isis, who has held my fascination since I was a boy. It sounds utterly ridiculous to relate such an experience, but in the realm of dreams, one can accept such fantasias without the taint of skepticism. Perhaps that is why reality makes one deny the existence of myth and magic and question any incident that defies rational explanation.

My dream Isis looked exactly like my beautiful Karamaneh, yet I did not recognize this fact whilst I dreamt. She was simply Isis, my goddess, the same woman who first stirred my adolescent heart when I would huddle under my blankets with the beam of the lantern light directed down upon one of my father's Egyptology texts.

The dusky hand of the goddess took hold of mine and we flew through the air as carefree as Peter and Wendy in Barrie's wondrous story. I knew no fear, only the exquisite exhilaration of sharing the skies with the birds as if we were a modern Icarus and Daedalus gliding toward the sun. I looked below and watched as the great city I knew so well and the neighborhood where I had first practiced medicine receded into the distance and the clouds closed beneath us.

Her grip was sure, but free of pressure. I did not perspire nor did my heart race. It was bliss. I was living the life of contentment I always dreamt of as we dived back down through the clouds. Suddenly, we were sweeping down among the busy thoroughfares and crowded streets of London Town.

We glided past Oxford Street and Regent Street. The Café Royal bustled with activity far beneath us. We looked down upon Fleet Street and soared over the very roof underneath which my recumbent physical form lay sleeping. Simpson's and The Savoy were now rearing up to capture our attention. Pope Street and Bell Yard faded into the distance. Finally, we came to rest before a storefront in The Strand that I had never recalled seeing in my waking hours.

"This is the shop of my father." Isis spoke in a shimmering voice.

I passed through the doorway in front of her. She vanished into the ether at the threshold of the musty curiosity shop, although I did not actually note her absence until much later. Broken statues and ancient tomes were overflowing wherever I turned. The ceiling was littered with suspended cages containing exotic birds of every kind. A startling brightly-plumed creature squawked, "The Devil has come for you," as I drifted toward the backroom which appeared, at a glance, to double as the proprietor's living quarters.

An impossibly old man with a long flowing white beard clad in crimson robes and crowned with a golden cowl sat behind a small round table with a crystal at its center. This was the father of the goddess Isis. The old man was thousands of years old. I was not told these things, but somehow the knowledge was given to me just the same.

*"You wish to marry my daughter?"*

He did not speak, yet I heard his words just the same.

"I do, sir," I replied in a tone that I hoped conveyed my earnestness.

*"Then, you would do well to recall the words of Saint Dunstan."*

No sooner had he spoken than I saw the words of Saint Dunstan written in the air before me! I cannot tell you in what script, only that it was not English, yet I understood every word I read! I stood in amazement as I looked upon the strange script. It read as follows:

*"I doubt as yet you understand what man and wife do truly signify. Yet I know you to believe, without doubt, that it is sulphur and mercury. That it may be, but certainly not the common variety. For mercury essential is the true and faithful wife who takes her own life to bring life to her child after first she receives her man. Her perfect love doth make her soon conceive and then doth she strive with all the force she can, in spite of love, of life him to bereave, upon which being done, then she will never leave, only labor kindly, like a loving wife, until once more she has restored him to life."*

He spoke not a word nor made any sign, yet somehow I was compelled to turn my gaze to the crystal before us on the table. At first, I saw only an inky blackness within the stone. Slowly, the shadowy clouds dispersed and I saw the old man's unblinking eyes staring out from the crystal into mine. I became lost within the stone and saw myself falling. Strangely, the eyes grew no larger. Perspective had become meaningless although I was aware that I was little more than a microbe lost in the vast ocean of those amazing eyes.

I heard the old man's voice. I remember all of the statements that he made, but I cannot recall the order in which they were spoken. It was as if I heard all of his words at once and was still able to discern their meaning.

*"As an Englishman born in the Land of the Nile, you have no claim to a home.*

*"My daughter shall bear you a daughter and, in time, a son.*

*"You must trust the one who speaks the name of a good little man.*

*"If you value your life, avoid that which is unclean."*

The sensation of falling seemed to produce no emotion. I am unsure at what point I became aware that the eyes in the crystal had changed. They were no longer the eyes of the old man whom I had met in the shop in The Strand. These eyes were of a deep green and burned with an intensity that was familiar, yet somehow just managed to elude recollection. I fought to recall where I had seen them before. I tried to concentrate, but could not as the vision of falling into those terrible eyes consumed my every thought. I struggled to make myself remember that I was only looking into a crystal and none of this was real.

No sooner did I complete this thought then a thin, filmy membrane passed over those terrible eyes. The membrane was eerily reminiscent of the eyes of a bird. I felt a wave of nausea overcome me and then, I heard him speak. It was not the voice of the old man in whose shop Isis had led me. I struggled to recall where I had heard that unsettling sound before. It belonged to another old man. Tall, gaunt, with a massive skull bereft of but the thinnest crown of white hair. He wore no moustache or beard. Yellow, wrinkled skin clung to his face like that of a decomposing skull. He bore a strong resemblance to the immortal Egyptian Pharaoh Seti the First who had captured my imagination when first I glimpsed his likeness in my father's study. His piercing green eyes; the thin, sallow, high-domed skull; and that sibilant, yet guttural voice belonged to only one man…Dr. Fu Manchu.

"My eyes are upon you always, Dr. Petrie," he said.

I opened my eyes from my terrible dream and looked up into the face of Fu Manchu.

## 7. PEACE FOR THE WICKED

"Where is Karamaneh?" I demanded.

I was staring into the eyes of the frail old man seated in the chair across from my bed. The hideous marmoset perched on his shoulder chattered angrily at me in response to my question. A quivering, aged hand reached up to delicately scratch the marmoset's cheek.

"You forget your manners, Dr. Petrie. Have you no words of greeting for the old friend who visits your home?"

A terrible smile tore the thin, deathlike layer of flesh that covered Dr. Fu Manchu's face as he spoke. I could have leapt from my bed and strangled the miserable life from his neck had not a soft, warm touch to my shoulder confirmed what my heart already hoped was true. She was with him.

I turned and gazed upon the sad-eyed face of the most beautiful woman I have ever known. Karamaneh was by my side. I melted before those sad cow eyes and those perfect lips that quivered in fear not for her life, but for mine. Soft ivory skin and hair as black as the ebony night shone in the faint light from the window and made me long to crush her in a tender embrace. We were together again.

The only woman I have ever truly loved was seated on the bed barely three inches from my side dressed in the skimpy, shameful garb of an Arab slave girl. My heart rejoiced despite the terrible circumstances of our reunion. I was elated to see her, but I knew she was Fu Manchu's lawful property and would suffer greatly if I dared to touch her.

It took all of my strength, but I turned aside from the woman I loved and back to the man who stood as the sole obstacle between us and a life of happiness. I felt a queer mixture of repulsion and adulation for the titanic intellect housed within that feeble, decrepit form. Fu Manchu's aged face resembled that of a poet whose muse was Satan himself. His very presence commanded attention and respect as much as it did fear.

"I do so regret having to curtail your slumber, Doctor." He purred like a kitten. "All good men need their rest, but unfortunately, you have once again involved yourself in my business and I cannot grant you the courtesy of a peaceful night's sleep. However, you may count yourself as most fortunate. Despite your continued interference, I am not yet prepared to discount your few exceptional qualities."

He paused as if expecting me to graciously accept this backhanded compliment.

"You are a gifted physician and a man of integrity. A trait, I might add, all too uncommon amongst your countrymen. In recognition of this fact, and by way of granting a special favor to Karamaneh, I impart the following words of advice: remove yourself from Reverend Eltham's affairs. Where you and Nayland Smith would seek for answers lie dangers so great that even I could not save you from them if I wished. There is far more to this world than either of you are capable of comprehending. You are young and impetuous, Dr. Petrie, and have unwisely chosen to cast your lot with a fool. If you value Nayland Smith's life, you will share my advice with him. You have been warned. I can do no more for you. Good evening, Doctor."

He gathered his robes together and reached for his heavy wooden walking stick as if he were about to rise from his chair. The marmoset clung to his shoulder as he began to move.

"Wait! Please, I beg of you! Hear me out!"

My head was a jumble of emotions, but I was determined to act.

"Nayland Smith will not rest until you are dead and the Si-Fan has been destroyed. That you must realize to be true. Despite our differences, I know you, too, are a man of great honor, Dr. Fu Manchu. Your word is your bond. Therefore, I propose a truce. Give me Karamaneh and I will see to it that you and your servants obtain safe passage back to China. You have my word none shall molest you."

He stared at me for a moment with those queer, inhuman eyes and then he threw back his head and laughed. The marmoset chattered along with him in mocking imitation of its master.

"You are but a schoolboy led about by his latest passing fancy. I come and go as I please. Your English laws mean nothing to me. None impede my passing and none need grant me protection. I answer to an older law. I serve a power that was already ancient when this island was ruled by noble savages instead of pompous kings and scheming queens."

My desperation grew as I felt Kara slipping through my fingers yet again.

"Kara and I are meant to be wed. Do not deny us this happiness. Restore her to me and I swear I shall never again cross your path."

My fists were clenched. I could hear my voice trembling with rage. I sought for some sign of mercy in those uncanny eyes of his, but saw only my own despairing visage reflected back upon me.

"The gnat promises to trouble the elephant no longer. Your bargain cannot be met. Karamaneh belongs to me. You have no claim to her. If I wished it to be so, I could have you in my power from this instant forward. The means exist, if I so desired, to correct the errors in your thinking by application of a device of my own invention that is currently housed in my humble laboratory not far from this very apartment. Then I should suffer no further inconvenience from your tiresome principles. Instead, I should find you an only too willing servant. Bah! It is clear from your expression I have wasted my time trying to talk sense to an Englishman. Generations of inbreeding have robbed you of all your higher faculties. If I were a more patient man, I would simply sit back and let your precious Empire topple under the weight of its own idiocy. Look at him, Karamaneh!"

He pointed at me and I was overwhelmed by the sheer magnetism the man possessed as I could think of nothing to say or do in my defense. I merely sat there and listened like a child. I listened to the man I recognized as my better.

"He is a lovesick puppy. He is not worthy of your affections. I came tonight to spare his life, yet he is only capable of insulting me in response. Do you still want this whelp for a mate? Speak, woman. Lest I remove your tongue as an example to your fellow slaves."

I turned to Kara. She lowered her head and would not look me in the eye.

"I abide by your will, my master," she replied in a soft voice.

Had she drawn a dagger from beneath her skirt and plunged it into my heart, she could have done me no greater harm. I was devastated.

Fu Manchu's mouth twisted in a ghastly smile.

"You see for yourself, Dr. Petrie. You fight for a hopeless cause. Find some frigid English girl to pass your nights with and look not to my household for companionship. Whether you heed or disregard my warning rests solely on your own head. I can afford to waste no further time with you."

As he rose unsteadily from his seat, he inclined his head. I detected a movement behind me and started to turn. I had but a glimpse of a powerful Nubian out of the corner of my eye when, suddenly, I was struck with a blunt object upon the back of the skull and knew no more.

## 8. A WINDOW TO HELL

"Petrie! Petrie! Are you all right?"

I felt like I had been thrown overboard as I rolled onto my back. The clouds dispersed and Nayland Smith's face came into view.

"Smith, is that you? Good God, you should be in hospital!"

The furrowed brow that soured my old friend's face gave way to a look of relief.

"Never mind me, it's you I'm worried about, Petrie. What the Devil happened to you? I found you lying there pitched forward on your face with a nasty lump on the back of your head."

I touched the area and winced in pain.

"It was Fu Manchu, Smith. He was here, in our apartment, last night. Kara was with him and…there must have been a dacoit or thuggee. I was struck from behind."

Smith rubbed his chin with concern.

"If it weren't for that bump upon your head, I would suspect this was all a dream. What happened, man? Tell me everything."

I sat up on the bed with some difficulty.

"I walked home from the hospital last night and fell asleep straight away. I had the queerest dream. I met the Egyptian goddess Isis in my dreams and she…it sounds foolish, I realize, but she took me flying with her…over the city."

Smith lifted an eyebrow.

I hesitated for a moment, well aware I sounded a right twit. "She took me to an old curiosity shop in The Strand. There was a man there...a fortune teller of some kind. He was her father."

"The man from the old curiosity shop was Isis' father?" Smith asked in disbelief.

"Yes, he told me my fortune. It was all very queer. I can't quite remember what he said. It's as if the memory is just there round the bend and I can't quite seem able to grasp it. Anyway, I awoke at some point and realized the old man in my dream was Dr. Fu Manchu. He came to give me a warning and you as well."

"What did he say?" Smith snapped.

"He told me to cease meddling in Eltham's affairs as it was more than either of us could handle and he wouldn't be able to protect us."

Smith laughed. "That is a damn queer dream, Petrie. Since when does Dr. Fu Manchu offer us protection?"

"Smith, I am quite sure it was no dream. He was here...the bump on my head should be proof enough."

Smith's brow furrowed as he frowned. "Proof of something, but exactly what is the question. I don't doubt your recollection of the events, Petrie, but Dr. Fu Manchu is a master mesmerist. It is possible your memory and what actually transpired are two very different things. All the same, I take this as a sure sign we are on the right path. That incident at Redmoat cost me valuable time. We must proceed with my original plan of action. We pay a visit to the offices of McBride & Valley. Get dressed, Petrie. We haven't a moment to spare."

"What, now? It's half past three in the morning!"

"No time for objections, there's a good fellow. There's work to be done. Now off with you."

Thus it was I found myself braving the cold night air at Smith's side once more. His recent injuries weighed heavily on him physically, but the man had the constitution of an ox and nothing would slow him mentally or curb his willfulness. The doctors at Charing Cross Hospital had been unable to persuade him to stay the night. I would certainly fare no better in trying to convince him to rest until morning before determining whether he was ready or not to resume his investigations.

McBride & Valley's offices were far from what I expected. Rather than occupying rooms in one of the countless buildings looming over Fleet Street, their place of business was a small house in Dartford where the two publishers also resided. As we stepped out of the cab, the driver looked at Smith and me as if we were both madmen to have travelled so far in the middle of the night. I was not prepared for the sight awaiting us.

The house was alive with lights and the sound of revelry. There were no immediate neighbors at the end of the lane. One could hear the sound of raucous voices and a queer sort of music that immediately recalled the trip to Morocco I had made with my father during a school holiday many years before.

Smith marched forward resolutely. I half-expected him to knock upon the door and introduce himself when he made an unexpected detour into the snow that covered the front lawn. Before I could call out to him, he had disappeared behind a large snow-covered tree. My heart beat furiously until after what seemed an eternity, I caught sight of him crawling along the second storey ledge until he had reached the corner of one of the massive windows from which the sounds of activity seemed to emanate.

I realized he was motioning me forward, so I hurriedly traced his steps through the snow. I pushed my way through the shrubbery alongside the house and found a footing in the brickwork. I marveled at Smith's agility in such a weakened condition as I found it more than a bit challenging to scale the side of the house in the cold frosty hours before the sun rose.

I reached his side at last. The noise from the house was maddening. There were primitive drums pounding and reed pipes quivering to attain ever shriller notes with each passing breath. I counted at least five players from the sound of it. Each of the musicians was creating a discordant cacophonous mess as they failed to play in anything approaching harmony. The voices were harder to discern amongst the chaotic music, but it appeared to be screams and gasps interspersed with peals of uproarious laughter. Smith bent his head round the window to have a look inside. His face went white as a ghost.

"Good Lord, Smith! What is it?" I cried.

He seemed not to hear me. He kept staring through the window as if transfixed by what he saw. Suddenly, he let his feet dangle from the ledge, dropping his head from view. He swung himself past me, ably clinging to the ledge I stood upon with only his hands supporting his weight. His years in the Burmese jungles had served him well. He pulled himself up to my level and bent forward and hissed in my ear.

"Take a look for yourself, Petrie, but I warn you it is a window into Hell."

I did as he asked and edged my way down the ledge to the window and peered around the sill into the house. What I saw shook me to the core. The room looked like something out of *Arabian Nights*.

There was a fountain in the center of the room with divans arranged about it. The reed players and drummers were revealed to be eight nearly naked savages playing on a small dais. The divans and the Persian rugs that circled the fountain were occupied by a dozen or so men…Englishmen…engaged in relations with what must have been 20 Chinese girls.

"Good God, Smith! It's an orgy!"

No sooner had I spoken the words then I felt Smith's hand upon my shoulder, pulling me backwards. We fell for but a moment before landing with a jolt in a bank of snow. My shoulder stung from the fall, but I was otherwise unharmed. Smith's hand covered my mouth quickly. In the dim light shining down from the window above us, I could just make out his face. A finger was raised to his lips imploring me to remain silent. I nodded my assent and he removed his hand from my mouth. He pointed forward in the snow and I realized he had spotted someone approaching the house.

I was now able to pick out the sound of muted footfalls crunching in the snow. The sound grew louder and I realized the unseen arrival was walking toward us across the lawn. The crunching noise ceased not more than six feet away from where we lay.

"Mr. Smith, Dr. Petrie, please…join us. I assure you it is warmer inside and you'll enjoy a much better view."

The woman's voice tinkled like coins skipping across glass. Even before I raised myself up off the ground, I knew who was standing there before us in the snow.

"Well, Miss Trelawney, we meet again," Nayland Smith said as he rose up from the snow and brushed himself down. "I trust you have none of your exotic pets with you tonight, hmm?"

"I wonder if I know what you're prattling on about this time, Mr. Smith."

She sighed with exaggerated irritation. Even the blistering cold could not dampen the woman's flair for the dramatic.

"I wonder if you wonder," Smith muttered. "Still, you said something about inviting us into a warm house. I don't know about you, Petrie, but I'm all for the idea."

The air about Smith was clouded with his frozen breath. He blew into his clenched hands for warmth before lending a hand to help me up from the ground. Without another word, Ursula Trelawney turned and stalked toward the front entrance to the house. She was dressed in beautiful furs with a smart little hat resting on an angle upon her head. I couldn't help but notice the furs only served to accentuate the natural curves of her body as she strode through the snow like a panther stalking its prey. Her hair appeared to be a reddish golden hue when before I would have sworn it had been a dark brown. She was truly a bewitching figure.

As we approached the front steps, the massive wooden door opened and we found ourselves facing an uncommonly short, squat man dressed in a tweed smoking jacket. His olive-colored face and heavy-lidded watery eyes suggested a hint of Mediterranean blood somewhere in his family's past. An odd half-smile creased his cherubic face.

"And what have we here, Ursula? Wayward souls seeking shelter for the night?"

His voice was elfin and rose with what sounded like amusement as he spoke.

Ursula Trelawney swept back her fiery golden tresses and leant down to kiss the repulsive little toad on the corner of his mouth.

"Nothing so melodramatic I'm afraid, Neville. These two gentlemen are those friends of Daniel's that I mentioned to you earlier."

His face brightened as he stepped forward to greet us.

"Ah, Mr. Smith! Dr. Petrie! How good to meet you. I am Neville McBride. The better half of McBride & Valley, I always say."

He reached up and grasped our hands with rough, gnarled fingers. The little man used surprising force. I felt sure he had crushed several bones.

"Come inside! Come inside! Warm yourself by the fire before you catch a death of pneumonia." His bizarre little voice rang out in excitement in the cold night air.

A few minutes later found the four of us seated about a roaring fire in the large sitting room just off the hallway. A peculiar sickly sweet smell permeated the house. I could detect no sound to indicate the frenzied scene Smith and I had glimpsed through the second story window. We sat silently on the settee opposite Ursula Trelawney and our host. I waited for Nayland to take the lead. An unsettling stillness hung about the place.

The briefest glance around the room was enough to tell one a small crowd had been gathered here quite recently. Books and papers were scattered about on tables and floors. Plates covered in crumbs, some containing half-eaten sandwiches were strewn around the room in shocking disarray. The settee was lacking a pillow and a heavy woolen blanket lay thrown over one of its arms.

"Is our arrival in any way inconvenient, Mr. McBride?" Smith asked with faux sincerity. "I hope we're not disturbing one of your private late night gatherings."

"Not in the least, not in the least, Mr. Smith." The diminutive man beamed at us. "The middle of the night is of interest only to thieves and lovers. You'll forgive me if I don't presume to which category the two of you belong?"

"Very witty," Smith chuckled amiably. "Is it original or something you picked up in the schoolyard?"

"Touché, Mr. Smith." McBride laughed good-naturedly. "Did I detect a childish jibe at my stature in your retort?"

Smith only smiled in return. We sat in uncomfortable silence for a few more moments. Eventually, I plucked up the courage to speak.

"We had a glance in your window just now..." Smith shot me a warning look as I spoke. "...and I would have sworn we saw a bit of a...a celebration going on upstairs."

"That's quite impossible, Dr. Petrie." Ursula Trelawney stroked the strap of her dress provocatively as she spoke. "Only a fool would have ventured to peer through a second story window on a cold winter's night and, in any case, this is hardly the time for a celebration. We are all grieving Daniel's tragic passing."

That she was lying, there was no doubt in my mind. That she knew we were aware of her falsehood was underlined by her taunting sarcasm. I sympathized with Smith's temptation to strike her a second time that night in Redmoat.

McBride broke the uncomfortable silence. "It is such a pity about Daniel...and how tragic he did not live to see his memoirs in print," he said.

Smith crossed his legs and cleared his throat in irritation. "Of course, had he not chosen to write that damned fool book of his in the first place, doubtless then he would still be among the living."

The little man looked ready to respond to Nayland when he sneezed several times violently. He pulled a black-stained handkerchief from his breast pocket and blew his nose with disconcerting force.

"Daniel spoke of the two of you often," he said as he wiped his mouth with the handkerchief. "You both play quite an important role in the latter part of his book. I also understand Daniel has likewise been portrayed in Dr. Petrie's stories so this should hardly come as a surprise, no?"

"I publish my stories under an assumed name and likewise protect the identity of everyone involved."

McBride smiled at me disdainfully.

"How very gallant of you, Doctor. Of course, fictionalized accounts should remain anonymous. Daniel's memoirs are quite a different beast and for the sake of integrity, he refrained from making any such concessions."

Smith cleared his throat again as he removed his briar from his breast pocket and began packing it as he spoke.

"Petrie's Yellow Peril stories are published with the blessing of the Home Office. They perform a public service by raising awareness of the ongoing threat facing the Empire, while revealing nothing sensitive that would jeopardize innocent lives by spurring the enemy into further action. McBride & Valley has deigned not to take such measures for Eltham's memoirs. I had hoped to speak with Eltham about this matter in person, but that is impossible now. I hope you will have the good sense to at least submit the finished manuscript to the Home Office for approval before seeing the title in print."

McBride grinned at Ursula as if Smith had said something amusing.

"I suspected that's what your making a nuisance of yourselves tonight was about. Let's not waste any more precious time, Mr. Smith. I have nothing but contempt for the Crown encroaching on foreign territories such as your beloved Burma. Why should I jeopardize my own livelyhood by involving myself in the affairs of nations Britain has affronted?"

Smith struck a match and held it close to his pipe as he spoke through clenched teeth. "Whether one desires to be part of this conflict or not is quite beside the point. Your involvement as Eltham's publisher makes it impossible to shirk your responsibility. The same cunning devil who sought to silence Eltham will not hesitate to do the same to you or your...lesser half." Smith let the sting of his suggestion hang in the air a moment before continuing. "Speaking of whom...I suppose Mr. Valley is upstairs at present?"

That unsettling half-smile returned to McBride's face. "I thought that question was already answered, Mr. Smith. The four of us are quite alone in the house. As to your other remark, I loathe cowardice. Daniel understood the risk he was taking by stepping forward every bit as much as Thomas and I did when we agreed to publish his book."

I cleared my throat, nervously. "*Man o' God* will be the first title you will have published not aimed squarely at the avid student of the occult. I'm curious to learn why you found the memoirs of a former missionary so fascinating?"

McBride seemed to obsess on a piece of lint on his lapel. He scratched at it compulsively. "You are correct in one respect only, Dr. Petrie. If the book merely recounted the exploits of a missionary in a foreign land, we would not be interested, but you see, *Man o' God* is a logical addition to our catalogue because it recounts Daniel's journey toward the esoteric truths of Gnosticism."

Finally satisfied with his lapel, he smoothed his jacket and shot us both a dull look. "As such, his life-changing experiences in China that shaped the man he became will be of tremendous interest to anyone with even a passing interest in the Black Arts."

Smith clicked his tongue reprovingly as he rose suddenly to his feet. "Since you've made it clear you will not willingly cooperate with the Home Office, there is little reason for us to take up any more of your or Miss Trelawney's time. We leave you to your orgy. My compliments to the Brotherhood of Magi for maintaining their self-control whilst we were here. I sincerely hope for all of your sakes that those lovely Chinese ladies entertaining the Brotherhood upstairs were not procured from a Limehouse tong associated with Reverend Eltham's murderers. As much as I've seen of Miss Trelawney, I have no wish to sully the memory by fishing her bloated, desecrated corpse out of the Thames or some other such undignified resting place. Good night to you both. Don't trouble to show us the way out. Come along, Petrie."

I was as startled as our host and Miss Trelawney by Nayland's abrupt dismissal. I quickly rose and followed him out into the hallway where he had already donned his coat and hat and was handing me mine by the time I reached his side. I gasped as I looked up at the painting on the wall above the coat rack. I did not recognize the artist, but it was awash in charcoal shades of grey, black, and brown as it depicted a Pagan orgy between men and beasts in a forest clearing. The swirling mass of clouds above this hideous scene were shaped to form the muscular torso of a man with the head of a goat overlooking the shocking episode with what one could only imagine was a look of perverted pleasure.

Smith grunted that he had already seen the portrait as he turned toward the door. My mind was reeling with countless questions, but the look on my old friend's face was enough to silence me for the moment. In spite of my curiosity, I left that hellish house with little regret and longed for a hot soak to cleanse myself of its stench once we were safely home.

## 9. GONE FISHING

"Inspector Dunbar and his men will oversee the raid on McBride's household." Inspector Weymouth nodded in the direction of his associate. "We should have the lot of these degenerates under lock and key by the time you're finished in Limehouse."

Robert Dunbar stood and pulled his derby down upon his brow. The bullish detective shook hands with Weymouth, Smith, and me and bid us good luck before setting out.

We had assembled in Weymouth's office just after five in the morning. Smith and I had not been to bed yet, nor had I had time for the bath I so badly needed. Smith had insisted we proceed immediately to Metropolitan Police Headquarters and arrange for a raid upon McBride's house for the unlawful activity being carried out there. Whilst this was underway, we were to make our way through the back alleys of Limehouse in search of information on who had provided the Brotherhood of Magi with the Chinese girls for last night's soiree.

"I'm certain there is some sort of connection to the Si-Fan, Petrie," Smith said as we set out from the station. "If we are fortunate enough to establish a link, it should be child's play to tie Fu Manchu to Eltham's murder."

"Is there any doubt in your mind that the Si-Fan is guilty of masterminding and executing the crime?" I asked.

"Of course there isn't," he snapped, "but this time, we'll make sure that fiend swings from the gallows. Every scrap of evidence we can lay at his feet will make our case that much easier."

"Smith, what if Inspector Dunbar and his men arrive at McBride's residence and find no sign of any inappropriate conduct? Then we'll have warned the enemy without achieving an advance."

"I've considered that, Petrie, but the enemy is already forewarned. Our presence there last night saw to that. Dunbar will at least bring McBride and the Trelawney woman in on the strength of our testimony alone. The important thing is that we are on hand in Limehouse before any link to the Brotherhood of Magi falls cold."

Less than an hour later, Smith and I began banging on snow-covered doors and ice-frosted windows seeking some sort of lead on an Englishman who had procured 20 or so Chinese girls of easy virtue. Three of Weymouth's best men with years of experience in the Chinese Quarter worked the opposite side of the street. By the time the sun had risen, we had been cursed at, spat upon, and drenched with the contents of a full chamber pot in the course of having disturbed at least two dozen sleeping Chinese families without having found any answers to our questions.

Limehouse was now buzzing with activity as street vendors began hawking their wares. Cats and chickens scattered about as heavy wooden carts rattled on the icy ground beneath their wheels. The sound of voices shouting in that same barbarous tongue rang out all around us. I was exhausted and frustrated and wanted nothing more than to go home. I suspected more than a few of the Chinese we spoke to were only feigning ignorance of English.

As the hours wore on, Smith and I decided to part ways and, in so doing, double our efforts. As Smith trudged off to the next street, I rested for a moment against a heavy wooden door. I was about to knock when it opened and I found myself gazing into a wizened old face.

"Oh! Pardon me. I was about to knock just now. I hope I didn't disturb you…"

The old Chinaman smiled sympathetically at me.

"I wanted to ask you if you knew anything about some Englishmen who had come to Limehouse for some…" I lowered my voice in embarrassment. "…for some girls, actually."

"Girls?" He repeated the word in a fashion that it made it unclear if he comprehended its meaning.

"Oh, God," I swore under my breath. "Yes, perhaps you've heard of the Brotherhood of Magi? They're a sort of secret society of…well, of bloody loonies, if you ask me."

The old man continued smiling at me. His eyes twinkled, but he gave no sign he understood me.

"Perhaps you've heard of Neville McBride?" I stammered nervously.

"Mick Bride?" He bisected the name as he repeated it.

I was about to give up and walk away when he stepped aside and motioned me to enter. Feeling unsure of whether I was acting wisely, I did as he directed.

"You have come about the Ghost Brides, yes?" He spoke in halting English. "You pay for procurement of the girls?"

"Chinese girls, we're talking about, right?" I asked nervously. I did not know what a Ghost Bride was and feared I had stumbled down a blind path.

The old man nodded eagerly. "China girls, yes." The word *girls* sounded like *dolls* as he spoke. "McBride want Ghost Brides. He promise not to spoil. He lie to Wal Tam. Spoiled girls no good for Ghost Brides. You pay for girls now."

The old boy was quite excited by this point. I wasn't sure what to do next. He was clearly just what Smith was looking for, but how could I extricate myself from this situation and reach him without scaring my host off?

"I don't have any money for…Wal Tam, was it?" I stammered. "If you'll let me find my friend, I'm sure we can…"

I broke off as the old man turned holding a butcher's knife in his trembling hand. He smiled menacingly at me and began to chatter like a monkey.

"No money for Wal Tam. No friend for you. You pay with your life, Englishman."

I backed up instinctively against the wall. My hand reached back and felt the wall was a door. Momentarily, I was aware of double doors swinging inwards against my weight. I stumbled backwards into darkness and realized I was falling into a pitch black cellar.

*Oh no, not again,* I thought to my horror.

I have no recollection of hitting the floor. I was only aware of blackness and an abyss before consciousness escaped me.

An image began to form in front of my eyes. I tried to focus on the blurred face leaning over me. My first recollection was of a wide grin and then of unsmiling eyes. A hairless head with skin as white as chalk pockmarked with crimson blisters was leaning over me. I gasped in spite of my training as a doctor. The man before me was the most grotesque victim of a fire that I had ever seen. Gradually, I realized that he was not smiling. The hideous grin had been carved into his face as a permanent leer. The eyes were all that was left of the man who once was.

Before I could speak, he withdrew from the room without a word. I could not shake the feeling he was grinning malevolently at me even though, as a doctor, I recognized the fact he could have no control over his facial muscles. My surroundings were sparse. I was lying on a cot in what appeared to be a simple cottage. I could only assume I was still in Limehouse.

A movement from the doorway took my mind away from the constant pain. Fantastic as it sounds, I saw my old friend Daniel Eltham enter and rush to my side. I knew I was seeing the impossible for Daniel Eltham was a dead man, but there he was in front of me just the same. He wore a worried expression as he grasped my outstretched hand.

"Dr. Petrie! I feared the worst. That was quite a nasty fall you took. You are most fortunate that I chanced upon you in the snow."

I was flabbergasted.

"What do you mean you chanced upon me in the snow? I was in Limehouse…how did I get here? Where am I?" I stammered hoarsely.

His brow furrowed as if he were deeply concerned by my words.

"You have suffered a concussion. You are delusional. You slipped on the ice and fell in the snow. You have been unconscious for many hours. You are fortunate I came upon you before gangrene set in."

He reached into his pocket as he spoke.

"Here, take this. I want you to keep it."

He tucked a small metal icon of an encircled star into my breast pocket.

"Whenever you feel distressed, I want you to remember the charm I gave you and call out in the name of God, *Bismillah*, and know that all is well."

"*Bismillah*?" I repeated.

"*Bismillah*," Eltham smiled reassuringly as he patted me on the chest.

He was quite right. I did feel more like my old self. I was no Believer and certainly not a Muslim, but there was an undeniable sense of comfort in thinking there was a powerful Father watching over me, protecting me. I laughed out loud for thinking this dream was real. I had fallen backwards when Smith and I were searching Limehouse and yet…something was not quite right. This was all too real to be a dream.

"Daniel…when I awoke just now, I thought I saw…a man…"

He smiled at my efforts to form this simple question.

"Yes, Dr. Petrie. I'm sure Kau gave you quite a fright. I'm sorry about that. He has quite a grisly visage I'm afraid. A bad accident a number of years ago took all the skin from his face and left his mouth somewhat badly torn. His own people drove him out to live among the beasts of the jungle."

"His own people, you said…is he a native of some sort?"

"Chinese. Kau is quite a common name among those damn queer people. He is trustworthy, though and possesses tremendous skill as a healer. You have him to thank for your remarkably speedy recovery."

I struggled to sit up.

"No, Doctor. You are too weak and Kau is very self-conscious about his appearance. He prefers to remain out of sight. Rest now for you will be safely back at your apartment soon enough. Rest and remember...*Bismillah*."

"*Bismillah*," I repeated.

I shut my eyes to the soothing feeling that all was well and no harm would befall me.

I awoke in darkness. I had no way of knowing how long I had slept. The feeling of calm serenity had deserted me. Where was I? I sat up and moved off the cot and stumbled to my feet. Had Eltham's ghost and that hideously deformed Chinaman abandoned me or had they both been part of my dream? If I had been dreaming, then where was I and how had I come to be in this place?

There was a doorway directly across from the cot. I was sure of it. Whether dreaming or awake, I had seen the Chinaman leave by it and Eltham enter from it. Arms reaching out in the darkness, I slowly made my way toward what I hoped was the right direction. No obstacles hindered my way and within a few steps, I had reached the doorway just as I had remembered it.

Once through the doorway, I froze for I had no way of knowing what lie beyond this point. There could be a descending flight of stairs or any number of traps hidden in the blackness waiting for me to blindly blunder into them. I held my breath and tried to listen. I could hear crickets chirping and the cold wind blowing. I was near an exit! I almost cried out with joy.

My heart was racing furiously. I reached a hand to my chest when suddenly I felt something hard in my breast pocket. It was the metal icon of the encircled star Eltham had given me! It hadn't been a dream. It was real.

"*Bismillah*," I intoned and repeated the word over and over again.

So intent was I upon the joyful discovery that I was not mad with fever that I stumbled forward in the dark. I had a strange sense of imbalance doubtless caused by the head injury that still throbbed with pain. My feet tripped over some unseen object. My footing gave way and I tumbled forward, scraping my head against what must have been a low ceiling.

That was when I saw the moon. I fought a wave of nausea as I felt myself spin through the night air. For the second time, I landed hard on my side as my right arm, ribs, and leg absorbed the force of the fall.

I was in a wooded area filled with the sounds of nocturnal life. It was cold both from the air above and the snow beneath me. Moonlight showed the way forward. Behind was blackness and uncertainty. I did not know how I had come to be here, but all that mattered was finding my way back. I pushed myself through thickets and branches until I reached a clearing. I had no way of knowing where I was and I didn't care. All that mattered was getting free of the black forest.

I ran as fast as my legs would carry me shouting, *Bismillah* at the top of my lungs. I was nearing a perimeter wall and could just make out a gate a few yards yonder. Tears streaked my face as I ran towards the entrance praying it wasn't barred.

*Bismillah. Bismillah. Bismillah. Bismillah. Bismillah. Bismillah. Bismillah.*

The word reverberated in my skull like a pounding drum giving me the courage to carry on. A torch beam caught me and I froze like a deer in its tracks.

"Great God in Heaven, its Dr. Petrie!"

I knew that voice. It was Inspector Weymouth!

The torch was lowered and I could make out the grizzled features of my old friend in the dark. I grasped him with both arms and tried to speak, but found I was still repeating *Bismillah* like a scared and senseless child. Slowly I quieted myself and broke into a sob.

"Don't try to speak, man. You're nearly frozen to the bone. Let's get a blanket round you. I have a good mind to half-throttle you for giving us the slip and coming out here on your own."

Weymouth guided me through the gates toward his waiting automobile.

"What the Devil did you think you were doing anyway? Why did you abandon Smith back in Limehouse?" He snapped.

"Smith is in Limehouse? I fell…" I mumbled.

"You're damn lucky that's all that happened to you. Never mind now. All's well that ends well, I suppose."

He shut me into the back of the cab and climbed in front. After a moment, the engine roared to life.

"There's important news, Petrie. Whilst we spent the better part of the last two days scouring Limehouse searching for some sign of you, Inspector Dunbar made a remarkable discovery at the McBride place down in Dartford."

"McBride's place… Inspector Dunbar was there?" I stammered, transfixed by the glare of the auto's lamplights on the blackened country road before us as we set out on the long road back to the city.

"Not when you were there! Good Heavens, you're a right mess! Dunbar conducted a raid on McBride's Dartford residence whilst you and Smith were searching Limehouse for those Chinese girls you saw at McBride's residence three nights ago. You do remember all of this, don't you?"

I nodded that I recollected the incidents as he described them. I was trying desperately to cling to my sanity. Something had gone dreadfully wrong and I was afraid to discover what it was that had happened to me.

"When Dunbar and his men arrived on the scene, they found the place deserted. It had been looted as well, regrettably. Windows busted. Furniture overturned... doubtless the work of the Si-Fan. Whatever incriminating evidence may have been inside the house had clearly been removed. Dunbar later recalled the presence of several snowmen on the front lawn, but he failed to consider it significant at the time."

*Oh God,* I thought. *Not more snowmen.*

"Had Smith and you been on hand, as you should have been instead of waking up every law-abiding John Chinaman in Limehouse and subjecting him to a lot of bloody useless questions, we might have found them sooner. In any event, we didn't know what had happened until some neighborhood children were out playing during the day. They noticed five huge snowmen on McBride's front lawn and, chancing no one was home, decided to make sport of it. You can imagine their shock when they pummeled the first snowman and found a dead body inside."

I fought back tears and fell back in my seat reaching for the metal icon when I felt something else. There were several pieces of paper folded in half pinned inside my jacket. Who could have done it and why? Luckily, Weymouth had kept his eyes on the road and had seen nothing.

"Little blighters scampered like gazelle before the lion when the constable came around, but we'll sniff them out soon enough on the off chance they have something to say that is worth noting. Smith is at the coroner's now to see if he can identify the bodies. I'd best take you along. He'll want to know you're all right. You may be of some use as well. Now…tell me what the Devil happened to you this time."

I struggled to collect my thoughts. How I could explain that which I didn't fully understand myself? That's what my father called the churchman's dilemma. I smiled at the memory and looked at Weymouth's expectant eyes reflected in the automobile's mirror.

"I was exhausted…still am, come to mention it…I fell behind while Smith went forward and…and…and I fell inside somewhere…a cellar, I think. I leaned against a door and it opened unexpectedly beneath my weight. The next thing I knew…"

I was unsure what had actually transpired when I recovered consciousness. I resolved to stay silent on the events with Wal Tam and the Ghost Brides until I had a better grasp of what was real and what was fantasy.

"I'm sorry, Weymouth, but the next thing I knew I was wandering around in that forest when I bumped into you."

Weymouth snorted derisively. "That forest, as you call it, is Redmoat."

I gasped at his words. My God! I had really seen Eltham's ghost in Redmoat!

"After I learned of the corpses that were uncovered on McBride's front lawn, I thought we might have missed a clue when we collected Eltham's body. Must have been your guardian angel drawing me back to that accursed estate or you would still be wandering around freezing your arse off."

Weymouth guffawed and shook his head.

"Sometimes, I wonder what you and Smith are made of. The falls and cuts and bruises you endure would be enough to stop an elephant in its tracks…or at least a giant snake."

I grimaced at his poor excuse for humor and fell silent for the rest of the ride. My curiosity about the papers in my pocket was itching badly, but I thought it best to wait until I had some privacy with which to review them by myself first before sharing them with the others. Had I been in my right mind or, at the very least, well-rested, I may have chosen to act with more prudence.

"Petrie! Thank God you're in one piece! You had me worried sick, old chum."

Smith embraced me warmly as I followed Weymouth through the doorway of the coroner's office. He held me at arm's length to study my face. His joy at discovering me alive quickly waned with his growing frustration at my feigned ignorance of the events that transpired in the time between my fall in the cellar and when I was found by Weymouth wandering around the grounds of Redmoat.

I was unsure if my encounter with Eltham and the horrifically deformed Chinaman had happened or if it was naught but a fantasia brought about by my concussion. Either way, my head injury was the root of my poor judgment. I chose to say nothing on this point or my visit with the wizened old Chinaman. I was not the least bit troubled about the mysterious icon, the strange Arabic word still echoing in my head, or the still unread sheaf of papers tucked safely away inside my jacket pocket. A man who is not in his right mind is liable to make many poor decisions. I had proved to be no exception.

Chalmers Cleeve escorted us to where the bodies were on display. The room was gripped with a dismal severity. The air was chill and motionless. When death comes unnaturally, there is a disordered aspect to the body's features even if the deceased did not meet with a violent end.

The five naked men lying grey and still before us recalled the appearance of Eltham's corpse. Their identities were completely unknown. The lifeless bodies lay there discolored and unmoving as if made of clay. They were the unclaimed dead and there was no one to grieve their passing. A clinical detachment was the only recourse left for those forced to deal with their unexpected and unwelcome intrusion upon the world of the living.

"We know a bit more this time than we did with your friend, Eltham."

Cleeve circled the five tables. His manner and voice were ghoulish. He had worked too many years among the un-living. I sometimes wondered if Smith and I were likewise being robbed of our humanity.

"Like Mr. Eltham, the five subjects before you give the appearance of bachelors. I am told your friend Eltham was a widower of a great many years. He did not wear a ring. You will note the ring finger on each of the five gentlemen here bears no discoloration from the absence of sunlight. The neatly manicured fingernails and toenails and the well-groomed hair suggest these were indeed gentlemen…quite likely businessmen given to travel who would not immediately be missed. Now I wish to draw your attention to the most salient point of comparison between the five men and indeed with the late John Daniel Eltham."

He paused to tap the forehead of the corpse closest to his left with a gloved finger.

"Note the irritated skin on the fingertips of each corpse. Despite the freezing temperatures they endured whilst packed inside snow and ice for several hours, the irritation did not subside and is evident still in death."

"By Jove, you're right, Cleeve!" I exclaimed.

"Have we ruled out poison?" Smith asked.

Cleeve slowly nodded his head.

"We've ruled out all the known varieties of poison, Mr. Smith, but given the fact that your fiendish Chinese friend is involved, I think it too soon to close that particular book."

Smith grimaced.

"That is not necessarily the only solution to the puzzle. Eltham had left the ministry and become embroiled in Theosophy. There is little way to know what sort of enemies he had made in the process."

Cleeve's mouth twitched as he stared off for a moment.

"That's a bit like saying he became a Freemason. Theosophy is far too broad to pigeon-hole. You're looking for a cult...something with rites that can be tied to similar deaths. Surely, your Chinese friend with the penchant for causing all sorts of strange deaths is the natural starting point."

"Agreed, but the Si-Fan prefers such deaths appear natural and this is a beast of an altogether different sort. Unless we find that they worship snowmen or polar bears."

Cleeve smiled slightly at Smith's gallows humor.

"That is where the humble police surgeon bows to the experience and dedication of an expert like you, Mr. Smith. Happy fishing, gentlemen. I hope you catch a whopper."

By evening, the newspapers were filled with the story of the Six Snowmen. My agent had left several messages for me to call. He was eager to know if Fu Manchu was involved and when I would have my latest story ready for the next issue of *The Storyteller*. I resolved to wait a day or two before responding. Whilst Smith enjoyed a warm bath, I unpinned the folded pages from the inside of my jacket and spread them out upon my bed. They were filled with Chinese lettering and geometric shapes that held no meaning for me.

Who gave me this and why? Did I accept it during my foggiest moments after the fall? More importantly, what value did it hold?

I resolved to fold the pages up and put them away when a premonition caused me to turn to the doorway. Smith stood there, wrapped in a bathrobe, wearing a sour look upon his face.

"I didn't hear you knock," I said crossly.

"I didn't hear you mention anything about those papers. Why were you hiding them in your jacket?" he asked quietly.

"You were spying on me!"

"Oh, stop being so melodramatic! You've not been yourself for quite some time now. Of course, I'm keeping close watch on you. Now answer the question…where did you get those papers and what do they concern?"

I stared at him a moment and then collected the papers and folded them along their crease.

"I have no idea. They were on my person when Weymouth found me. That's all I know. Take them. See what you can make of it."

He took the papers, but didn't break eye contact with me.

"You need a rest, Petrie."

"I intend to do just that after I bathe and I daresay I need that even more."

"That's not what I mean. You need a break from all of this. It's wearing on you. You're a doctor, not a detective. It was unfair of me to expect more from you. I'm booking you passage to Paris in the morning."

"Paris? Why should I go to Paris?"

"We need to get you out of the fray for a bit. You need time to recover before you get back into the thick of things again. Don't look so glum, this isn't permanent. Fu Manchu is lying quiet at the moment. If anything stirs up while you're gone, I'll wire you. Besides, you can be of greater use to me there than here."

"What's in Paris?"

"Not what, Petrie, whom. The answer is Greba Eltham or will be soon enough. She is booked on the 10:30 Folkestone Express tomorrow and so are you."

"Greba! What? How long have you known of this? Why didn't you tell me sooner?"

Smith chuckled and clapped a hand on my shoulder.

"Which question would you like me to answer first? You forget you've been out of commission for the past two days. Much has happened, but the affair of the Six Snowmen has certainly overshadowed the rest. Weymouth tracked down Greba. She took the news of her father's death rather badly as one would expect. Weymouth asked her to stay available in the coming days as there will likely be more questions the further we delve into the matter. That's when Gaston Max entered into the picture."

"Who the Devil is Gaston Max?"

"Monsieur Max is the most brilliant detective in the world, if Inspector Dunbar's estimation is anything to go by. He's worked with him in the past. Gaston Max is with the French Sûreté Nationale. He was contacted by Greba to investigate a suspicious foreigner who was involved with her father. Yes, I thought that would catch your attention. The interesting thing is that Greba asked Max to meet her in Paris and informed him she was leaving tomorrow. Happily, Dunbar was able to speak with Max and information was shared on both sides. Through Max, we are able to arrange a coincidental meeting for the pair of you. Had you not turned up, I would have been forced to go in your place. Your task will be to keep close tabs on Greba and find out all you can about this mysterious foreign friend of her father. Gaston Max, understandably, is unable to dedicate his full attention to the matter. Obviously, we have no desire to forcibly detain her unless it becomes absolutely essential that we do so."

I felt more alive than I had for some while.

"A foreigner, you say? I hope this Gaston Max is up to the task if the Si-Fan is involved."

"He has had some experience with our Chinese friends when he assisted Inspector Dunbar a few months back on the Mr. King affair. He has also dealt with a local terror of such unspeakable deviltry it made our Fu Manchu business look like child's play in comparison."

"Good Heavens! Are you sure this trip is going to constitute a holiday for me?"

Smith chuckled. "The madman I refer to went down on the *Titanic* along with my brother and two of France's bravest men, one of whom was a close associate of Gaston Max."

"I'm sorry, Smith, I didn't mean to…"

"It's all right, man. You couldn't have known. Great tragedies take the good with the bad. Death does not judge a man by his merits, only his place in time. Now start packing before I change my mind and go in your place. A holiday in Paris with a girl as pretty as Greba Eltham is certainly no chore."

## 10. NAME OF A GOOD LITTLE MAN

I took the 10:30 Folkestone Express from London and boarded the ferry to cross the Channel. I had not seen so much as a glimpse of Greba Eltham and had concluded Weymouth's information must have been wrong or else Eltham's daughter had made an eleventh hour change of plans. In any event, I slept peacefully on both rail and water as I was terribly exhausted from all that had transpired this past week. I stumbled aboard the train at Calais in a near somnambulistic stupor. My black mood was gradually bringing me out of my sleep-induced daze. I barely recalled handing the conductor my ticket when a voice startled me from my reverie.

"Dr. Petrie!"

I turned and saw a pretty young woman had pulled aside the curtain to my compartment and was standing there staring at me with a surprised look on her face.

"Greba!"

Nayland Smith had intended to manufacture our crossing paths, Greba had simply made it easy for me by finding me first.

"Oh, Dr. Petrie, have you heard...?"

I nodded my head yes. Standing, I took her hands in mine and offered a few trite words of consolation. She buried her head in my chest and sobbed.

"It's as if it were all some awful nightmare. I keep expecting to wake up and find everything has gone back to the way it used to be, but the nightmare never ends. Father was such a fool. I know it's terrible to say at a time like this, but it's the truth. Those friends of his were just using him."

She looked up at me as she spoke. Her eyes were hard and cold. All of the softness I was accustomed to finding there had turned to stone.

"They killed him. I know they did. I haven't the proof, but I'm sure of it. Say you'll believe me. I need someone I can trust."

I held her at arm's length and asked her to start from the beginning. She took a moment to compose herself and asked if she could sit down. We sat across from one another in the cramped berth.

"It all began about 14 months ago when Father first met a man called Fulton Denison. He was a penniless drifter with nowhere to go and someone in the neighborhood sent him our way. You know what Father was like. He took him in, fed him, bought him a set of clothes, and gave him some money to make a new start...just as he had done so many times before. But this man Denison wouldn't go away. He was different from the others. He had a darkness about him that unsettled me. He always seemed to be watching me. When I told Father that he made me uncomfortable, he chastised me for judging him. Denison began to dominate the conversations at the dinner table with his queer talk of philosophy and what was best for mankind. It sounded all right at first I suppose, but the more he talked, the more concerned I became."

"Concerned in what way?" I asked.

"He seemed to exert some sort of influence on Father. His opinions became Father's opinions. His moods became Father's moods. Father became very short-tempered and black. He only smiled or laughed when he and Denison were speaking in private. It was a hard laugh, not like Father at all. Oh, I know you must think me a silly little fool for saying such things…"

"Dear, nothing could be further from the truth. I know precisely what you mean. Now please, go on with your story."

She tried to smile for a moment, but the tears would not be contained.

"Oh, Dr. Petrie, why did Father have to change? Why couldn't he be with me now? He said such hateful things to me. I told him I would never forgive him, but I do forgive him, I do. He's gone and I'll never be able to tell him how sorry I am…how much I loved him."

I held her close until her sobbing subsided.

"Did this man Denison introduce your father to Neville McBride and Ursula Trelawney?" I asked.

She pulled back with a start and stared at me for a moment.

"I have no idea. I've never heard either name before. I know Mr. Denison was using Father's money and resources to contact a great number of people... they could have been among them, I suppose."

"What sort of people?" I snapped.

She shook her head for a moment as she searched for the right words.

"Like-minded people, I imagine. It was all to do with that philosophy he was always on about. When Father walked away from the ministry, it was the final straw. I left home. I wasn't going to stand there and silently condone his squandering his life's work. All of his possessions and savings were being controlled by Mr. Denison. He was going through Father's money so quickly that Father was forced to dismiss Edwards and the rest of the staff. It was an untenable situation and I could do nothing except sever all ties with him."

I shook my head sadly.

"If you'll forgive my asking such a delicate question at a time like this, did your father adequately provide for you?"

Her eyes grew wide as she looked up into mine.

"There's nothing left...nothing at all. Father gave everything away... all of it."

She squeezed my hand after a moment's reflection and looked down at the floor.

"I realize I have no right to ask for your help..."

She studied my face as she spoke.

"Oh, please, don't think its money that I want, Dr. Petrie! It's not, I assure you. If you're going to Paris, well...I wondered if I might join you. I realize it's highly improper, but the gentleman in my compartment...he's very kind, don't misunderstand me...but, I think he has designs on me and that's the last thing on my mind at a time like this."

She spoke in a quiet voice so devoid of emotion that I couldn't help but smile. "You know that I would go to the ends of the Earth for you, Greba. My compartment is empty. You are welcome to join me for as little or as much of the time remaining as you like. In the meantime, we'll run along to your compartment and let you introduce me to this young man of yours. Once he sees there is an old family friend on board, he'll soon look elsewhere for companionship."

"Thank you so much, Dr. Petrie. I knew that I could count on you."

She favored me with a radiant smile.

"Oh, Mr. Pethig, this is Dr. Petrie. He's an old friend of my father's. He'll be looking after me while I am in Paris."

I was more than a bit taken aback to discover Greba's Mr. Pethig was anything but a young man. He was a middle-aged gentleman with a shock of prematurely white hair encroaching upon a widow's peak. A sparse white goatee lent an air of sophistication and professionalism upon haggard features that betrayed a weakness for the bottle. He nodded to me curtly and then immediately directed his attention back to Greba.

"Well, I trust you will at least still deign to dine with me, Miss Eltham. I've taken the liberty of ordering for us both while you were out. We should be served momentarily. Had you told me you were meeting a friend on the train, I would have...but perhaps the doctor already has plans of his own for dinner, yes?"

I smiled at the fellow's rather obvious suggestion that I was most unwelcome.

"On the contrary, I would be delighted to join you for a little conversation. I'm not the least bit peckish and I would certainly relish learning more about you, Mr. Pethig. Needless to say I am very appreciative of your being so kind to Greba."

I motioned for Greba to sit next to me as I sat opposite this rather unpleasant man. She looked nervous, but no less uncomfortable than Pethig at my intrusion. I had taken an immediate dislike to the man. He was far too old to be forcing his attentions upon so young a girl as Greba. I glanced at his hand and noted he wore no ring. There seemed to be a rash of unmarried gentlemen about lately. I needed to be rid of him quickly as I could not afford to waste unnecessary time once we reached Paris.

The porter served their dinner shortly. As expected, there was a moment of anxiousness as the boy insisted I must order something as well. I assured him I was not hungry and, taking her cue from me, Greba left her plate covered and excused herself for not having much of an appetite either.

My mind was wandering and I found my gaze drifting out the window as the trees rushed by as the train hurtled down the track. I was vaguely aware of Pethig admonishing Greba for not eating and I faintly recall hearing the clinking of metal as Greba uncovered her plate. I glanced down the table when I stopped short with a start. The *entrée* she had just uncovered was a pork loin. The very moment I laid eyes upon it, I heard the words of the old man from my strange dream a few nights ago repeated in my head:

*"If you value your life, avoid that which is unclean."*

"For the love of God, Greba, don't touch the pork!" I shouted.

Forks and knives clattered loudly on the table as Pethig and Greba gaped at me in utter astonishment. I quickly took up Greba's utensils and hurriedly sliced through the meat.

"Dr. Petrie, have you taken leave of your good senses?" Greba hissed.

I had no idea how I could begin to explain my irrational outburst. I began to consider the possibility that I was suffering from mental strain when a queer gurgling sound interrupted my thoughts. Pethig sat across from us, his face a bright purple. Protruding eyes watered profusely. Bits of meat fell from his mouth as he sputtered and coughed.

"My God, he's choking!" Greba shouted. "Dr. Petrie, do something!"

I was rooted to my seat. The hairs on the back of my neck were standing up. Against all of my years of training, I was unable to make a move to help save a dying man's life.

The terrible gurgling sound continued as spittle formed around Pethig's mouth. He flung himself forward onto the floor of the compartment and crawled on his hands and knees as if in some sort of frenzy. His strength gave way after a few paces and he collapsed with his head resting on its side just inches from my feet.

Forcing myself to act, I knelt beside him and loosened his collar rapidly. I felt for a pulse, but already knew that there would be none to find. Strangely, his neck and face were bloated and the purplish hue had not abated, but instead seemed to intensify until finally, those horrible tear-filled eyes violently burst from their sockets in a storm of blood and mucous. I was vaguely aware of the sound of Greba gagging. I was numb to the horrible scene as my mind returned to that strange dream of mine once more.

"Its poison, isn't it?" Greba asked, breaking my concentration.

I nodded my assent as I stood and sat next to her in the booth.

"Look at the meat on your plate. Note that peculiar, nearly colorless powder just visible where I sliced the pork open. That is not seasoning. The same powder can be seen on Pethig's fork and knife. If he had paid as much attention to his plate as he did your *décolleté*, he might still be alive. I trust you'll forgive my bluntness under the circumstances."

I knelt back down to the dead man and cautiously examined his body. As I worked, I noted Pethig's forehead, still a burning purple hue, was hot to touch. The horrible, empty eye sockets appeared to contain ammonia amidst the bubbling blood and pus. I was careful not to touch them for fear that I would share his horrible fate.

"I need to get my bag," I told Greba as I stood up. "I am not sure what to make of this. It is certainly a poison of a variety that I have never before encountered."

"That poor man..." Greba said.

"Doubtless, we have Dr. Fu Manchu to thank for this welcome. Well, I'm glad to see that you had not yet started on the main entrée yourself."

"Thanks to you, I hadn't. I must admit I thought you were out of your mind when you spoke up just now. How on Earth did you know something was afoul with the pork loin?"

I sat back down with a heavy sigh and collected my thoughts for a moment before I told her of my bizarre dream. The more I spoke, the more I was sure I had only convinced her that my sanity was still in question until I mentioned the old man's jumbled predictions of my future:

*"My daughter shall bear you a daughter and, in time, a son*

*"If you value your life, avoid that which is unclean.*

*"You must trust the one who speaks the name of a good little man"*

"The name of a good little man!" Greba spoke the words as if they were familiar. "The gentleman I'm meeting in Paris, Monsieur Gaston Max of the Sûreté, always says that queer expression."

"Gaston Max!" I said in astonishment.

"Oh, you've heard of him? He is said to be one of the most brilliant men in the world. He's very definitely bright, but I find him to be rather eccentric...he has a whole battery of funny French expressions at his disposal. My favorite is *nom d'un petit bonhomme*."

Greba affected a heavily accented baritone for a somber reading of the phrase before breaking into a delightful series of giggles.

"*Nom d'un petit bonhomme… Name of a good little man.* You must admit, it's all quite deliriously funny. I'm sorry, I know this is a terrible time to laugh, but it's the first time I've laughed in weeks."

I was grinning from ear to ear with relief. It seemed my queer dream was actually prescient. I was pleased to find Greba returning my smile with renewed assurance. Under the circumstances, I thought it best not to reveal the other details of the dream or my knowledge of her meeting with Gaston Max. But I could not get Dr Fu Manchu's words out of my head:

*"My eyes are upon you always, Dr. Petrie."*

Indeed, they had been this evening.

## 11. DARKNESS ABIDES

"Lord Almighty! What happened to Mr. Pethig?"

The porter's question was not an unreasonable one and should have been expected. However, it was most unwelcome when one is passenger aboard a train bound for Paris and discovered kneeling next to the corpse of a fellow passenger. Greba nervously cowered in the corner of the berth.

"He's been poisoned and Miss Eltham very nearly shared his fate." I spoke with the calm measured tone of the professional physician and hoped I sounded reassuring. "Where is your cook?"

The boy seemed quelled by my demeanor.

"I... I think I'd best get the conductor," the porter stammered.

He returned moments later with a white-faced conductor. Both men were eager to prevent the spread of hysteria aboard the train and were more than willing to maintain their discretion until the authorities in Paris could be advised.

I explained who I was and repeated my question about the cook, but the conductor told me he'd gone missing. He never took his eyes off Mr. Pethig's corpse.

"What exactly happened to him, Doctor?"

I glanced down at Pethig's horribly contorted face with its ghastly empty eye sockets.

"He ingested poison. Poison so potent it caused his eyes to swell and burst within minutes. I'm sorry. I realize this is not a pleasant sight. Murder never is pleasant. I don't wish to appear crass at the scene of a tragedy, but I have every reason to suspect Miss Eltham was the actual intended victim and that Mr. Pethig was merely an unfortunate casualty. You mentioned the cook has disappeared. Do you mean to suggest that he was the victim of foul play or does it appear that his departure was planned?"

"I... I don't know." The conductor stammered.

He glanced at the porter who nodded his head in agreement. The men appeared perplexed for the moment as if the latter possibility had not crossed their minds. I asked if the conductor objected to my having a look at Mr. Pethig's belongings. He said he supposed it was all right provided he was present to witness that nothing was removed from the compartment.

There wasn't much to tell. Keenan Pethig travelled light. Apart from his passport, there was precious little apart from clothing and toiletries to distinguish him. I could make no guess as to the gentleman's profession or his reason for visiting Paris. Leaving the porter behind to guard Pethig's body with strict orders that no one be allowed to touch the food on either plate, we followed the conductor to the kitchen area.

The cook was a man called Kane Keller. A portly German émigré who kept to himself much of the time and seemed disinterested in forming friendships; he was considered a short-tempered man best avoided by the rest of the staff. Unsurprisingly, the kitchen area provided no clues of any significance

"When was the last time anyone saw Herr Keller?" I said.

The conductor shrugged. "I asked around the train... No one seems to have seen him since early this morning."

"Did this man have a known residence in either Paris or Calais?" I asked.

I waited whilst the conductor checked. He returned shortly with a Paris address for an apartment near the waterfront.

Our arrival in the city entailed the expected questions from the station officials, but once I produced a telegram from Inspector Weymouth confirming my identity and noting that I was currently engaged on official business for the Crown, Greba and I were free to go. I left the name and address of the hotel where I would be staying.

There was no question of letting Greba wander off on her own now that an attempt had been made on her life by the Si-Fan. As she had not yet booked hotel accommodations for herself, I offered her the safety of sharing my room. Paris was not a city to frown on assignations and Greba knew me well enough to know that my intentions were strictly honorable. She had said nothing more of her planned meeting with Monsieur Gaston Max, but I reasoned I would learn everything in due course. I trusted Greba instinctively and saw nothing in her actions to give me cause to doubt her.

No sooner had our interview with the authorities concluded then we took a cab to the waterfront to have a look at Kane Keller's apartment. He resided in an old crumbling building that marred an otherwise magnificent view of the Seine. The landlord was easily bribed with a few *centimes* and led us to Keller's room and unlocked the door after knocking several times and receiving no answer. He hung back behind us I suspected, not in fear we bore ill will towards his tenant, but in the hopes it might profit him another *sou* before we were finished.

The apartment appeared vacant. There was no sign of the German. The bed was neatly made. The entire room gave the appearance that no one had stayed in it for quite some time. I ran my finger along a bureau and watched it trace a heavy line through the dust.

"How long did you say it had been since you had seen Monsieur Keller?" I asked the landlord in French.

The ugly little man grunted. His nostrils flared as he pursed his lips and twisted them into an unpleasant scowl.

"Not this long. From the looks of it, he has not slept here in quite some time."

"Then why would he continue to pay rent?" Greba asked me in English.

"Because he wished to give the appearance he was sleeping here in the event anyone inquired after him," I replied.

I pulled open the drawers of the bureau. They were filled with neatly-stacked clothing. I dropped to my knees and peered beneath the bed. There was a wooden chest wedged underneath it. Gripping the box with both hands I tugged until it came free. I flipped it right side up and was grateful to see there was no lock.

Inside the box were a number of papers covered in symbols. Upon closer inspection, the symbols appeared to be line drawings of a table of some sort. There were no words on the pages, making their value to the bearer all the more puzzling. I set the papers aside as I noted several photographs in a pile beneath the papers. Carefully, I withdrew them from the box.

I recognized a considerably younger Keenan Pethig in several of the photographs. Another man appeared in many of the photographs; some with Pethig, some without. He was bespectacled with a thin Aryan nose. He looked to be about 40 years old with dark curling hair that crowned his high forehead. Heavy jowls that elongated his face. Considering the additional weight he carried, I considered I may have misjudged his age by anywhere from five to ten years. I tossed the pile of photographs back inside the chest, snapped the lid shut, stood up and pushed it with my boot until it disappeared beneath the bed once more.

"There's nothing more for us to learn here, Greba," I said. "Thank you for your time, Monsieur."

"Did those old photographs of Mr. Pethig tell you anything?" Greba ventured to ask as she sat down next to me on the settee.

"Well, he had some sort of connection to the mysterious cook aboard the train where he was killed. I am quite certain it was he that we saw in several of those photographs with Pethig. I suspect they were both rather unsavory types. We may never know the real circumstances behind his death, but I'm beginning to suspect the incident had nothing to do with you at all. It could have been a simple case of blackmail or a gambling debt or revenge… There may be a woman involved somewhere, who knows? In any event, Dr. Fu Manchu appears to be innocent of all wrongdoing for a change. I happily leave this business to the local authorities to sort out. I think it quite possible that we'll not be troubled by any of this again."

We had dined before checking into the hotel. Being alone with Greba, even under such dire circumstances, was still a bit disconcerting. Greba shivered and withdrew from me. It was evident she was shaken by all that had occurred and my presence alone was not enough to reassure her. I put a comforting arm around her shoulder.

"Don't worry, dear. I've been knee-deep in ghastly business like this for the past three years. You'll be safe enough in my care."

She frowned as she listened to me.

"It's not that, Dr. Petrie. I've been more places than most girls my age, thanks to Father. I've seen good men die through both fair means and foul. Death is the fate awaiting everyone in the end and there'll be no avoiding it when it calls for you."

"I must say you make for cheery company tonight," I chuckled.

She stood and walked over to the bed across the room and sat down. I watched her as she moved and felt a sense of dejection at the distance she chose to place between us.

"I wouldn't blame you if you wished Nayland Smith were the one looking after you right now rather than me. He's certainly the better man when it comes to navigating rough waters such as you've found yourself."

"Why must you always do that?" she snapped irritably.

"What do you mean?" I asked.

"You're always so hard on yourself. Come here."

I rose and did as I was bade and sat down next to her on the bed. She grasped my hands as if she were speaking to a child.

"You do just fine under duress… far better than I could manage on my own."

She paused for a moment and then smiled fondly at me.

"I've never properly thanked you… I've read all of your stories… I was very…flattered by your description of me."

I felt the blood rush to my cheeks. I had given little thought when writing that I would be judged on how I depicted the events and people who had played a role in the Fu Manchu adventures. Sitting on a bed in a strange hotel in Paris with the young woman I had described as a classical beauty at my side only magnified my discomfort.

Greba glanced down and smoothed the bedspread between us with her delicate fingers.

"There is one thing that has always puzzled me. If you honestly meant what you wrote about me, then why did you swoon over that treacherous Egyptian slave girl?"

She was staring at me now with eyes that had suddenly turned to stone again. I felt strangely guilty as if I had somehow wronged her by falling in love with Kara.

"She tried to kill you and Nayland Smith at least half a dozen times. She serves that awful Chinaman… I'm… I'm sorry. I have no place judging anyone. Father was right. It is one of my failings."

Her gaze returned to the bedspread, but this time her hand shook as she fought to control her emotions.

"One doesn't choose who one loves." I quietly said.

She looked up at me sharply with eyes ablaze once more.

"Don't be daft. Love is a choice as sure as anything else in this world. I don't pretend to understand why you would choose her and I certainly don't understand why you let your heart be ruled by someone you may never see again. You behave as though you were a widower when it's patently obvious you the two of you have never been…"

I was stung by her words and spoke sharply as a consequence.

"Is it any different than letting your will be overruled by a God who may not even exist? Imposing laws and limitations that prevent you from enjoying yourself?"

Greba's lips parted slightly as if she were ready to reply. I wondered momentarily if she were about to counter with some argument learned in years past from her father before all thought of Reverend Eltham vanished from my mind as I leant forward and kissed her.

Greba mumbled vague words of protest and half-heartedly beat at my chest with her tiny fists as I gently lowered her backwards down upon the bed. Presently, her protestations ceased and there was only the sound of warm rain upon the window sill above us to blanket the soft murmurings of two lovers who lay just out of sight.

## 12. MIDNIGHT IN THE CITY OF LIGHT

I awoke to thoughts of Kara. I felt remorse for my actions... even more so because I was genuinely attracted to Greba. The emotional distance I sensed between us last night before we made love had become a permanent barrier upon waking in one another's arms. I am a poor conversationalist at the best of times and this was certainly not one of them.

It appeared I had failed some sort of test by initiating the release that we both so ardently desired. Consequently, Greba had little more to say to me and certainly showed no interest in demonstrating anything approaching affection. Perhaps it would have been different had I pledged my love to her afterwards, but we both knew she could never mean as much to me as Kara regardless of what had happened.

We retreated to separate hotel rooms that day, albeit across the hall from one another. I sat in my room and stared at the blank sheet of paper in front of me. There was much I had yet to commit to print of our recent exploits with the Si-Fan, but as the hours ticked by, the sheet of paper remained pure and unblemished, unspoiled by my vile hands.

Where had I gone wrong? I had always been a sensible lad and certainly not one to be made a fool of by every pretty face that happened by. I had maintained a respectable practice before Nayland turned up again after all those years away. It was as if I was finally given a second chance to enjoy what I had missed during my childhood.

My father may have been a great man, but it certainly wasn't easy being his son. All of his passion and enjoyment were wrapped up in a mummy's tomb. I tried to immerse myself in his texts when I could, but invariably I was just in his way. It was far easier to ship me off to school than to deal with a motherless boy. It was far simpler for me to pretend both my parents were dead.

Smith had always been the model schoolboy. Studious and athletic, there was little doubt he was destined to achieve greatness. Now nearly three years had passed since he had burst back into my life bringing excitement and danger with him at every turn. I had loved every thrilling second spent by his side, but in the end, I was just as ill-suited to his way of life as I was to my father's.

Kara was beautiful and I longed to love her as I had no other woman before and yet, I was no hero. I couldn't save her. I may have won her heart, but I couldn't win her freedom. I would be better off returning to Cairo to search for the lost treasures my father loved than to vainly search the world for the treasure I loved but had lost. I knew full well I could never keep hold of either of them for very long.

Smith was right as always, I was better off forgetting Kara. I should follow his example and swear off women. I wasn't a swashbuckler any more than I was a Romeo. I was respectable and it was time to put away my childish dreams and accept myself once and for all before my reputation was beyond salvaging.

That night, I sat alone in my apartment, silent and brooding, and smoked my pipe while I ruminated over the Six Snowmen, Keenan Pethig's tragic fate, and that mysterious prescient dream that was never far from my mind. If Pethig's death was unrelated to the Si-Fan, how did Fu

Manchu know to warn me about the poisoned food? Was I mistaken and Greba's life was spared only through a remarkable coincidence?

My father had raised me to be a skeptic and, like him, I was possessed of an inherent distrust of my fellow man and a pronounced disdain for the inexplicable. The one exception in all things was my friendship with Nayland Smith. I wished he were there to guide me now, to take the responsibility for choosing which path to follow, but he was back in London and I was alone with my actions and naught else to blame for their consequences.

Smith was the best mate I ever had. Our friendship was the only thing he truly believed in, apart from the Crown. I often wished he would welcome some fleeting female companionship to relieve him, if only temporarily, of the tremendous burden of having dedicated his life to destroying the Si-Fan. Smith never had much use for women despite his rugged good looks. There had been some sort of brief love affair some months back whilst I was in Cairo, but it had ended badly and left Smith even more committed to living a life of solitude.

He mistrusted women as a rule, but chose to keep such thoughts to himself most of the time in deference to my feelings for Kara. I respected him all the more for the restraint he was capable of exercising. A restraint I could never hope to emulate having been a slave to my volatile emotions since adolescence. I could imagine Smith even now, standing in the doorway watching me, knowing my every thought.

"You can't sleep, can you, Petrie? You keep thinking of that poor blighter, Pethig," I could hear him say. "You'll feel better after you've met with Greba's famous Gaston Max. He'll soon sort everything out."

"Dr. Fu Manchu has haunted my life like a specter these past few years. Sometimes it's hard to believe he's actually a living, breathing person," I spoke in a soft, quiet voice more to myself than to my imagined companion. "It's almost comforting to wake up knowing there is one man who is responsible for all that is wrong in the world. Of course, Dr. Fu Manchu is a genius of such mind-boggling magnitude it makes it difficult to muster the strength to carry on fighting against him. If only there were some means of reaching him... of converting him, why, there would be no end to the good he could accomplish."

"Stop it," I could hear Smith snap at me. "Fu Manchu wouldn't stand a chance on our side and we both know it."

"Why?" I asked. "Why must it be so?"

"He's a Chinaman, Petrie; he'll never be anything better. I thought the same as you once, but circumstance demands we set aside Queen Victoria's lofty idealism and accept the fact that the dreams of that Great Lady whose heart loved all are most emphatically not shared by the vast majority of the Crown's subjects. We need our villains to play the part of the scapegoat. We hate them for what they reveal about us. They are the sacrificial lamb needed to stave off the darkness within our own souls."

I knew Smith was right. We were doomed to engage Fu Manchu in battle for no better reason than he was a Chinaman and we were Englishmen. The future I dared to dream for myself meant a life of exile in Cairo where Karamaneh and I would be accepted, albeit begrudgingly, as husband and wife. My beloved England would only offer us the coldest of receptions, as Kara would always be looked upon as a heathen foreigner.

I smiled as Smith's voice and image faded from my mind and I knew I was very close to total exhaustion. I extinguished the lights after undressing and got under the covers. Despite my weariness, or perhaps because of it, I found myself restless. I lay awake for what seemed like hours thinking of Greba and remembering her touch, the smell of her hair...

I had finally dozed off when a sudden shiver disrupted my slumber. I was instantly alert as though I had received a subconscious warning. From the unexpected chill and the sound of rushing air, I quickly deduced my window was open. I could just make out a shadow-shrouded figure standing next to my bed. As I watched, my brain raced to consider my next move when both of the figure's arms rose above the shadowy head without a sound. Instinctively, I rolled to the right and slipped off the bed.

There was a noise like rushing wind when a force emanating from the opposite side of the bed pulled the tangle of blankets from my body. Before I could react, the blankets fell to the floor around me, in shreds. Without thinking, I quickly regained my feet and grasped the empty pitcher of water from the night stand and hurled it in the direction of my attacker. An arm was instantly raised in defense and the pitcher clattered harmlessly to the floor. The movement revealed more of my assailant's silhouetted body and I realized, much to my surprise, that the intruder was a woman!

I darted round the side of the bed and locked both arms about her whilst she was distracted. She snarled savagely and lashed out at me with her feet. I squeezed my arms tighter beneath her heaving chest and tilted myself backwards until she was lifted bodily at least a foot off the ground. The witch leant forward and bit viciously into my forearm while continuing to kick away at any target within reach.

I fell to my knees by the side of the bed after she delivered a particularly vicious blow. She sprung from my arms toward the open window. I steadied myself against a hard, wooden object and grasped what felt like a thick club sticking up from the center of the bed and wrenched it free. It was an axe! She meant to kill me!

I stood to see her disappear out onto the ledge in front of my window. I quickly pulled my pajama bottoms on and followed her, axe in hand. The second I stepped onto the ledge, a dizzying wave of nausea overcame me as the wind pushed me flat against the brickwork. I looked down to the ground far below, and then out at the sleeping city resting quietly beneath the inky black clouds. I was frozen in the cold night air. Fighting to keep my balance and still my racing heart, I began to edge cautiously along the ledge in the direction that the she-devil had disappeared.

"Look out!"

I reacted to what I swore was a voice calling out a warning to me only to see my would-be assassin crouched down on the ledge at the corner of the building prying loose a crumbling brick. Steadying herself, she pulled back her arm to hurl the masonry at me. I raised the axe in front of my face as a shield, blocking my view of her. The brick struck the axe-head with such force that it nearly succeeded in dislodging me. I stood precariously clinging with one hand to the window pane. I could not get a good look at the woman's face as the wind blew her hair and robe about, but there could be little doubt that my assailant was none other than Ursula Trelawney!

"I won't hesitate to use this, Miss Trelawney," I warned as I hoisted the axe above my head.

She crouched down again and began prying loose a second brick in response to my warning when the corner of the ledge began to crumble beneath her feet. I gasped in fear as she scrambled to secure her footing. Frantically, I began edging toward her, desperate to reach her before she fell.

I stretched a hand out to her. She was just out of reach and would not turn her face up to look at mine. I glanced at the still crumbling ledge and tried to calculate how many seconds remained when, suddenly, an ear-splitting shot rang out and she toppled backwards off the ledge. Letting go of my hold, I dived to reach her and found myself falling forward into space.

I had just enough time to shut my eyes and let my muscles relax as I struck the roof of a neighboring building not 12 feet below. I lay there for a few moments until I ascertained that, although badly bruised, no bones were broken. I struggled to my feet and took hold of the axe that had landed just inches from my grasp. The crumpled form not more than ten feet away from me was of the woman who very nearly brought my life to a premature end. She lay on her stomach; I was not sure whether she was still breathing. I made a move toward her when I was grasped by the shoulder from behind.

"Who the Devil?" I cried.

"Non, *mon ami*, I am not the Father of Lies."

I gasped as a torch snapped on illuminating the unfamiliar face of the man standing behind me.

"Lay down your axe, Englishman. I am no more the criminal than you."

The speaker was a small-boned Frenchman dressed in an immaculate checked travelling coat. He held a small pistol in his hand, pointed at my chest.

"Monsieur Gaston Max, I presume?" I said.

"It seems you have heard of me, *mon ami*," he said with a gracious bow. "I am flattered."

"I am Dr. Petrie. The woman you just murdered was called Ursula Trelawney."

I gestured with the axe toward where she lay.

"You misjudge me." The little Frenchman laughed as he replaced the revolver in its holster. He reached for a small cigar from a pack concealed in the breast pocket of his coat and lit it. "Do you really think I would shoot to kill without first giving fair warning? And such a beautiful woman! *Morbleu!* Examine her, Doctor. You will see it was the concrete I shot from under her feet, in my desperation to save your life."

I cautiously knelt down to her side where she lay, face down on the roof. Placing the axe on the ground next to me, I gingerly turned her over. Gaston Max followed behind me and held the beam of his torch upon her face. I started as I found myself looking not into the unconscious features of Ursula Trelawney, but of Greba Eltham!

"*Eh bien!* This is not your Ursula Trelawney is it, *mon ami?*" Gaston Max asked.

I shook my head no.

"Guided by a good little angel we are tonight," Gaston Max cried. "*Sapristi!* I know this because the woman before you is none other than my very own client. *Mais oui*, it is clear that she was not in her right mind this night. It is most fortunate you are a light sleeper and I a stealthy tracker. Tell me now that the good Lord does not work in the mysterious ways, eh? Well, *mon ami*, we must get her to the hospital, but first, we must find you some more clothes. You must be freezing in this night air."

Somewhere nearby, a clock began to toll 12 times in the most remarkable city in the world. Amidst the chimes,

I would have sworn that I could hear peals of laughter and the chattering of a marmoset.

## 13. CAGLIOSTRO'S HEIR

"This young woman," Dr. Marat said, gesturing toward the unconscious form of Greba Eltham. "She is not the villain you seek, but rather, the victim. This young lady has fallen prey to the power of a mesmerist." The elderly Frenchman smiled. "Never fear, she will recover shortly and become her old self once more."

I was greatly relieved by the doctor's assurances, but more than a bit confused on how such an awful thing could have happened to Greba in the first place.

"However, you must continue to exercise extreme caution," Dr. Marat continued. "The man who has done this terrible deed has controlled her mind in some fashion. Perhaps by the programmed use of a word or a phrase or perhaps the sound or sight of an object... something that compels her to behave in so beastly a fashion towards those for whom she cares the most. The process could easily be repeated if you do not first determine the cause and prevent its recurrence."

I hadn't even the slightest notion as to when or how Greba had been hypnotized. Several hours had passed between the time when we had retired to our separate rooms and when she climbed in through my window with the hotel's fire axe in her hand, intending to murder me in my sleep. There would be no means of ascertaining what had triggered this transformation unless I witnessed it myself.

"Think on it no more for now," Dr. Marat said. "She must sleep and so should you, but bear my words in mind for tomorrow and do not let your guard down for even a second."

I looked down on Greba's peaceful face before leaving her side.

"So, my young friend," Gaston Max said to me as we left the hospital, "I take it that your holiday in Paris with Miss Eltham has not turned out as well as one might have hoped?"

"Far from it, I assure you. Although I fear to think what may have happened, had you not contacted Inspector Dunbar."

"*Oui*, fortunate we were in that respect. Dunbar is a good man. We worked together on the Yellow Claw case some months ago. He told me of you and your colleagues' involvement with this same group and the mastermind behind it. When Miss Eltham contacted me about a suspicious foreigner, and her fears that this man had played a part in her father's mysterious death, I felt obliged to break her confidence and share the information with him. I am glad I have done so, although I do not take the betrayal of a woman's trust lightly."

I cleared my throat nervously, unsure how the dapper Frenchman would respond to my pressing him for further confidential information.

"I have only the sketchiest details of what Greba has told you of this foreigner. She spoke to me of a man called Fulton Denison having aroused her suspicions, but she mentioned nothing about him being foreign nor has she professed to have any knowledge of the individuals we suspect have run afoul of the Fu Manchu group."

"And who are these suspicious individuals, Monsieur?" he asked.

"Neville McBride and Ursula Trelawney. The former was her late father's publisher; the latter his mistress. Both are tied to a theosophical sect called the Brotherhood of Magi."

Gaston Max stopped in his tracks and turned and looked at me severely. The calm and peaceful disposition that seemed to possess him most times instantly drained from his face.

"This theosophical sect you speak of, it is but a new name for an old idea. Your words suggest to me that there may soon be more victims added to this case. This is most troubling indeed."

"Monsieur Max, I do not speak with certainty. The ways of Fu Manchu are shrouded in confusion and deceit. Had you been with us in London and seen what we saw with our very eyes…"

He held up a hand to silence me. "I have said your words trouble me, but I did not say I doubted you. You must understand something of human nature, *mon ami*, before we are to proceed. Man is the same everywhere. Frenchman, Englishman, African… Only his skin may change, never his heart. Man seeks to invent reasons to set himself above his fellow men. One nation bests another. One religion bests another. The circle keeps multiplying, and yet it grows smaller and smaller with each revolution. A circle of those in a privileged class… A circle of those with special knowledge…! *Sapristi*! Hidden knowledge… Gnosis… That is what we are dealing with in the study of theosophy, *n'est-ce-pas*? Arcane knowledge handed down through the ages with a promise of what, hmm? Transmuting gold or discovering the secret of immortality, eh? They all seek freedom. Freedom from what, you ask? Morals… freedom from the Church who tells us we should be ashamed of ourselves. Licentiousness and knowledge... they are the tools of power and in the hands of man... vain, selfish man... they are the tools of evil. That is human nature, *mon ami*. That is the history of our world in but a few short sentences, eh?"

I couldn't help but think Monsieur Gaston Max was accustomed to dealing with people less clever than himself. Like so many otherwise brilliant men, he was prone to make sweeping generalizations. The kernel of truth contained in his philosophy seemed to reveal more about his own arrogance than it did anything else. His suggestion that the Holy Mother Church was above reproach only illustrated the narrowness of the Roman Catholic point of view.

"Might I ask the name of this foreigner you were investigating and how it relates to Greba's decision to come all the way to Paris just to see you?"

He smiled benignly as if I were a simpleton.

"The trouble with names is that one is as good as another."

It was apparent the man had no intention of taking me into his confidence just yet.

"I assume you would have no such trepidation sharing what information you do possess if you were dealing directly with Police Commissioner Nayland Smith or Inspector Weymouth of the C.I.D. rather than a simple English doctor?"

"Oh, please, do not take offence, *mon ami*. It was not my intent to insult you. We are colleagues, brothers-in-arms no less. Come, let us enjoy the night air and we shall speak on this in more civilized surroundings."

"Might I ask where we are going, Monsieur?"

"Ah, the eternal question... *Quo Vadis*?" He laughed cheerily. "I can think of no place more appropriate than your charming hotel, eh? The guilty man always returns to the scene of the crime, *n'est-ce-pas?*"

I was silent the rest of the way to the hotel. We climbed the stairs to the fourth floor and made our way to my room. As we reached the door, Gaston Max reached out a hand to caution me. He placed a finger to his lips as he pointed with his other hand to the apartment across the hall where Greba had stayed last night. The door was ajar.

I was not troubled by this fact as I assumed it was only the maid come to change the sheets on the bed, but Gaston Max brandished his revolver and was cautiously creeping forward. I followed a few steps safely behind him. From the open door, I could detect the sounds of papers being shuffled and then the scrape of a heavy piece of furniture being shifted. Without warning, Gaston Max burst through the doorway, pistol at ready.

"Halt! Keep your hands where I can see them, Monsieur. I will not hesitate to shoot."

A grey-haired man was stooped over the desk opposite the bed which had been pulled some inches away from the wall. Cautiously, he lifted his arms and stood straight. He appeared alarmed, but in no way menacing to judge by the laugh lines that ran deep into his thin, pleasant face.

"Might I ask who you two are and just what you think you are doing here?"

He spoke with an unmistakable English accent and was clearly a gentleman. The expense of his suit and his distinguished bearing suggested that he was a man accustomed to giving rather than receiving orders.

"I am Gaston Max of the Sûreté. Who are you and why are you in Miss Eltham's room?"

The thin, grey-haired man sighed in exasperation. "My name is Thomas Valley. I am a publisher. Miss Eltham's father was one of my clients. I have not forced the door. See for yourselves. The concierge willingly gave me the key. My partner recently severed all ties with the firm and I was hoping Miss Eltham might have a copy of her father's manuscript among her belongings. It is my rightful property under English law."

I was dumbstruck, but Max was still treating the man with suspicion.

"How did you come to learn that Miss Eltham was in Paris and why did you not contact her when she was in England, if she has papers that are rightfully yours?" he asked.

Thomas Valley sighed again with escalating frustration. "I contacted her a few days ago when we were both still in London. It seems her father died recently and the matter had attracted a police investigation, yet she told me she could not possibly be troubled to look through his personal effects as she was leaving immediately for Paris. I could not fathom how anyone could leave the country when their father had just been murdered, unless they themselves were fleeing justice. Still, it was none of my affair apart from trying to reclaim my rightful property. I should note that I fully intend to publish the manuscript as it may help recoup my losses."

"I find it very peculiar a publisher would not have more than one copy of a manuscript that he intends to publish on file," Gaston Max sniffed disdainfully.

Valley rolled his eyes in exaggerated irritation. "Yes, that makes two of us. I find the whole business peculiar. I have never even set eyes upon this fabled manuscript. It was entirely my partner's affair and he was insistent that it would make us both wealthy men. You should understand that the publishing business is not as straightforward or simple as one might imagine. Each time I tried to get a look at this magnificent manuscript that he kept raving about to me, he would manage to stay just one step out of reach. First, he was in Wales, so off I went to Wales. Then, he returned to London, so I followed him there. I could never run him down. He kept promising to post a copy to me, but he never kept his word... about anything, really. He regularly came up short and I kept finding myself having to forward him funds to cover his expenses until finally, I decided that enough was enough."

"You appear to have been an extraordinarily patient man, Monsieur Valley," Gaston Max said sardonically.

"Yes, well, when one has been partners with someone for nearly 20 years, a fair amount of due consideration is only to be expected. But even I have limits to what I am willing to tolerate. However, to the matter at hand... I arrived in Paris hoping to meet Miss Eltham. Instead, I find that she's in hospital and that, once again, it is a police concern. Not wishing to involve myself any more than is absolutely necessary, I asked the concierge if he would be willing to give me 20 minutes to ascertain whether my property was among her belongings. Fortunately, the man proved to be reasonable and I was able to persuade him to lend me a key. Now that I have told you everything, might I please put my arms down? I am growing quite weary of maintaining this dreadful posture."

"And did you find what you were looking for?" Max asked, ignoring his request.

"Not as such, but I did find a letter that had been posted to her by my former partner. It was lying open on this very desk. Curious as to its contents, I took the liberty of picking it up just before you entered. That, gentlemen, is the only questionable act I have performed, and even then, I believe I acted with sufficient cause."

"I see no crime in your actions. What did the letter say?" Max asked.

"I hadn't the time to read it... You don't mind if I lower my arms now, do you?"

Valley did so without waiting for Max to answer. He reached into his breast pocket and took out a folded piece of paper. His face remained impassive as he unfolded it.

"The letter contains only a single word. It's handwritten and there is no signature or date upon the page. What's even more peculiar is the fact that it wasn't written on our office stationery."

"What is this singular word?" I asked.

Valley paused for a moment and sucked on his lower lip in thought. He was a delicate fellow whose good looks and unnaturally black eyes were marred only by a slightly haunted expression. The fullness of his lips suggested miscegenation somewhere in his family's recent past. Their prominence served as an unexpected attribute as they softened an otherwise cruel mouth.

"It's a foreign word and I'm loath to say it in case it's something rude. Here, you can have a look for yourselves if you like."

He passed the letter to Gaston Max. The dapper Frenchman glanced at it, shrugged, and then passed it to me. I took the paper and nearly fainted when I saw written in the center of the page was the Arabic word: *Bismillah*.

In the name of God.

"Do you by chance know of a man called Fulton Denison?" I blurted the question at him without thinking.

"Yes, as it happens I do. He was an acquaintance of my former partner. In fact, it was he who arranged Neville's introduction to J.D. Eltham."

Valley's tone was genial. I was shocked by the significance of what he had conveyed. Here was proof at last that the man Greba was convinced had killed her father was also tied to the Brotherhood of Magi. The question that needed to be answered was, where did Dr. Fu Manchu enter into the equation?

Gaston Max looked at me and frowned before directing his own question to Mr. Valley.

"Are you also familiar with a Spaniard by the name of Esteban Milagro?"

"Esteban Milagro?" Valley repeated the name as if mystified. "Esteban Milagro is the greatest Adept alive today. He is the true heir of Cagliostro. There are many among us who would gladly sell their soul to Satan himself for the privilege of being called his disciple."

Upon completion of that amazing testimonial, the delicate and dashing publisher's eyes rolled up into his head and he fainted dead away.

## 14. A CHINK IN THE ARMOR

"Well, of course he fainted," Gaston Max snapped irritably. "I saw him with my very eyes."

We had carried the unconscious form of Thomas Valley to my apartment across the hall and laid him to rest upon the spare bed.

"You misunderstand me. I realize we both saw him lose consciousness, but I tell you the man is under the same hypnotic influence as Greba Eltham. It is exactly as Dr. Marat described. Valley lost control of his will before losing consciousness as a direct result of the same hypnotic force that commanded Greba to kill me."

"You are trying to convince me of the impossible, Dr. Petrie," Gaston Max sighed, waving the piece of paper in question in front of me. "We have no means of proving this letter holds the key to Miss Eltham's murderous actions the other night."

I reached into my breast pocket and removed the star-shaped metal icon.

"This is all the proof that I need. This icon was given to me by Miss Eltham's father. He told me to always keep it on my person and to repeat the Arabic word *Bismillah* whenever I felt distressed."

Gaston Max stared at me in silence for what seemed an eternity. I could not tell whether he believed me or thought me a madman. It would have been so much worse had I told him I had not actually encountered Eltham, but his ghost. Finally, Gaston Max broke the silence and spoke.

"I do not understand this. If you are correct and you have been hypnotized as well, then what effect is evidenced in your own behavior?"

"I cannot say for certain, but it is clear that we have established a pattern. Dr. Fu Manchu warned me to avoid becoming involved in Reverend Eltham's affairs. We believe that Eltham's manuscript holds the key to Fu Manchu's true identity and could very well expose the powers behind the Chinese secret society, the Si-Fan. You have promised to share more information with me. There can be no more delays. Too much is at stake. You must tell me everything. Perhaps when all the facts are laid before us, the truth will begin to fall into place and we will understand what connection the Brotherhood of Magi has with these events."

"I have already told you the name Miss Eltham gave me." Gaston Max snipped off the tip of his cigar and clenched its end between his perfectly straight, sharp little teeth. "The Spaniard, Esteban Milagro, is the man we seek. I cannot say why she told you the name of this man, Fulton Denison. Perhaps she was already under the influence of this unknown mesmerist and was deliberately deceiving you."

He struck a wooden match against the side of the oak desk and puffed away contentedly as the tip of the little cigar began to glow, sending billowing clouds of aromatic smoke around my room.

"The mesmerist is Dr. Fu Manchu; of that, there is no doubt in my mind," I said. "The question is, why and for what purpose? He has already silenced Eltham. If Neville McBride is one of his minions, then there would be no difficulty in suppressing the manuscript or at least removing any compromising details. Yet, that isn't what is happening here…or is it? McBride told Smith he planned to publish the book and yet Valley claims his partner has become unreliable and is trying to keep the manuscript out of his reach."

Gaston Max slowly shook his head.

"Surely your English law provides legal remedy in such an instance. If this Mr. McBride published Eltham's memoirs on his own, then Mr. Valley need only bring suit to halt its publication or, at the very least, claim his rightful share of the profits. I do not know whether we are confusing a simple matter of bad faith between businessmen with something more sinister, or if we have been deceived by all involved as to their true intent. In any case, I see no proof of a direct link between Miss Eltham's condition and Mr. Valley's outrageous behavior."

"Is there nothing more to tell of this Spaniard then what Valley has already said?"

Gaston Max bristled at my question. "I do not recall making any statement about Esteban Milagro whatsoever. As it happens, I have been concentrating my efforts on apprehending the gentleman in question for several months now. Following the recent upheaval in the French underworld, he has emerged as the new mastermind behind *Les Apaches*."

"What the devil have Apaches to do with the French underworld?" I asked in wonderment.

"I speak not of the Red Indian tribe of the New World, Dr. Petrie, but of their namesake. *Les Apaches* are thugs from Montmartre whose savagery bears comparison with the most fearsome native tribe of our former colonies. There are many such gangs in Paris... You have doubtless heard of *Les Vampires*, no? I had been involved in the hunting of the murderous fiend who led these gangs. He is dead now, thank God, but I fear he now has a successor. The man I now seek is called Esteban Milagro."

"This is the man Greba mentioned when she contacted you?"

"Yes, and as it also happens to be the name of one of the most wanted men in all of France, it attracted my attention. I do not know this Fulton Denison she spoke of, but it is possible he is an associate or an alias of Señor Milagro. The trouble is, Miss Eltham was only seeking information regarding this man, whereas my interest is in those who can lead me to him. However, given the fact that the Mr. King case pointed to a larger conspiracy centered on, but by no means limited to, the Chinese communities of Paris, London, and San Francisco, and given the fact that Miss Eltham and, more importantly, her father were, at one time or another, targets of this same criminal organization, I naturally suspected that some connection exists between this larger organization and *Les Apaches*, particularly if this man Milagro is involved with the both of them."

I considered all that he had said for a moment.

"It is more likely that the Si-Fan is using this man Milagro and his gangs to further some end of their own. The Si-Fan is much more than a mere criminal organization, it is a political movement. They mean to reshape the world and despite all our efforts, they are succeeding. The secret war that is being waged is one that we are fated to lose. These people use terror rather than armies to gain an ever stronger foothold in the West. They win more hearts and minds each day, while we are busy celebrating a burned base of operations or the arrest of a few worthless underlings as a victory. We are fighting a cultural battle and we are losing because we make no new converts. The Si-Fan's greatest strength is that the majority of the world lives in blissful ignorance of its power, or denies that it even poses a threat. Since I began publishing my Yellow Peril stories, I have been accused of hate-mongering against innocent people. No one, not even Nayland Smith, clearly sees this is not a war against China, but something far larger encompassing many nations. It is a threat that if left unchecked has the power to sweep the globe."

I sat back in my chair. My brow was covered in perspiration. I cleared my throat nervously as I tried to still the racing pulse that was throbbing in my ears.

"As I have said, we have made an important find. We possess the very clue that Dr. Marat told us to seek," I said. "He cautioned me that when Greba recovered consciousness, she might still be susceptible to hypnotic influence. He said that we had to do our best to determine by what means the suggestive force on her mind had been activated. That letter Valley discovered contained the answer!"

"*Bismillah*?" Gaston Max asked. "What is this *Bismillah*?"

"It is Arabic for *In the Name of Allah*," I answered. "I say again by means of this very word, and that queer icon that I showed you before that, I was likewise hypnotized."

Gaston Max shook his head in bewilderment.

"My friend, I fear that you are too excitable. There may be something in what you have related, but I know not the players or their motives. It may be that you were in fact hypnotized that night. It may be that part of your memory has been hidden from you, or that you have been made to believe that you saw Miss Eltham's father when, in fact, it was the face of another."

I thought on this for a moment.

"Perhaps you are right, Monsieur Max. Perhaps it was Dr. Fu Manchu manipulating me. He certainly possesses the mental powers to accomplish such a feat. I recall seeing a Chinaman that night. He was hideously scarred. Eltham—at least I thought it was Eltham—told me that the Chinaman had been badly burned in a fire many years before."

Gaston Max nodded slowly. "Your subconscious mind was beginning to resist. He had to act quickly to allay your suspicions and lull you back into a passive state."

"I don't understand… Why wouldn't he simply kill me? Why go to the trouble of hypnotizing me if I was already in his power?"

Gaston Max shrugged. "Obviously you are more valuable to him alive than dead. Had you not reappeared, your friends would have kept scouring Limehouse for you and perhaps found something else instead."

I nodded in agreement. This certainly sounded reasonable. I was finally gaining an appreciation for the Frenchman's skills as a detective.

"Of course, there is another possibility," he said warily. "You may yet have a role to play as the pawn of this master gamesman."

"Then, why set Greba upon me? For what purpose are three people hypnotized only to be set against one another?"

Gaston Max smiled. "Have you never played chess? Pawns are easily discarded. Your worst flaw, Dr. Petrie, is an inflated sense of self-importance. I pray that it does not prove to be a fatal flaw. We must be productive, Doctor. One way or another, Esteban Milagro is the man that we seek. Find him and we find your Dr. Fu Manchu."

"I don't suppose either of you have bothered checking the Masonic Lodge in Montmartre?"

We both glanced in shock at the bed. Thomas Valley was sitting up and staring at us.

"Are... are you all right, Mr. Valley?" I stammered.

He stared at me and blinked rapidly several times. "Considering the fact that I find myself in a strange man's bed, I suppose it could be said that I'm doing as well as could be expected."

Gaston Max rolled his eyes in irritation. "He's certainly not hypnotized now. As to your suggestion, Monsieur Valley, it is not very likely that it is the Freemasons that we are seeking."

Valley swung his legs off the bed and stood uncertainly.

"I claimed nothing of the sort, Monsieur Max. I only mentioned the Masonic Lodge in Montmartre because the Brotherhood of Magi has been known to assemble there. Surely, you are aware that the Freemasons will rent their Lodge to unrelated organizations? Any smart businessman would do the same."

Thomas Valley looked about my room as if he had misplaced something.

"Any chance of you letting me back into Miss Eltham's apartment? I'd like to finish looking for that manuscript."

Max and I stared at him without saying a word.

"Didn't think so, but I thought it was worth a chance."

Max rose up from his chair and took a threatening step towards the publisher.

"Monsieur Valley, if you have information regarding the Brotherhood of Magi you wish to share, then I suggest you do so. I haven't the time or the patience to allow you to exercise your theatrical ambitions at my expense."

"Very well, Monsieur Max, if you insist. It is a fact the Grand Orient of France harbors the Brotherhood of Magi when the latter assemble in Paris. It is also a fact that Esteban Milagro is a member of the very same Lodge."

"Explain your basis for making this claim," Max snapped.

"I have seen him there myself," Valley replied.

Gaston Max strode up to him and stared at the man in evident ill humor. "What business brings an Englishman to the Grand Orient of France, Monsieur?"

"Look, I'm simply trying to be helpful as it's painfully evident that neither of you really know what the Hell you're talking about. If you would like to gain admittance to the Brotherhood of Magi, I can bring you in as Initiates on my recommendation. There is little need for banging on doors and serving writs, or whatever you call them over here. You want an audience with Esteban Milagro and I can arrange that for you as well. It's really quite simple."

Max stared at the man.

"Where can we meet this man, Milagro?"

Valley smiled. "Wonderful, we have a date. Tonight at seven. The *Lapin Agile*. He will be hosting one of his little soirées, and I promised I would be there. However, I must insist you two be initiated into the Order of the Brotherhood of Magi beforehand. We will meet at six. The Lodge is located on the Rue des Abbesses. You will learn that there is much more to Montmartre than the Moulin Rouge and the Sacré-Coeur. Good day to you both, gentlemen."

Without a further word, Thomas Valley turned and walked out of the door.

"What a bizarre fellow!" I exclaimed.

"Yes, he is," Max drawled, "and a dangerous one."

"I can't imagine why he would want to help us."

"I thought that should be obvious," Gaston Max replied. "The Brotherhood of Magi is in trouble, so he first seeks to win our favor."

"What puzzles me is a member of one notorious secret society being willing to betray a member of another secret society that is hosting his brethren in Paris. That would seem to go against the grain of all they supposedly represent."

Gaston Max shrugged. "There is always a chink in the armor, provided one knows where to look."

## 15. THE GRAND MAGICIAN

Tea-time found Gaston Max and me strolling about the 18th *arrondissement* of Paris. Montmartre rests comfortably on its hilltop perch over 300 feet above the rest of Paris. The view of the city below is nothing short of breathtaking.

"Montmartre's name is derived from the Mont des Martyrs. The martyrs in question were Saint Denis, Friar Rustique, and Archdeacon Eleuthère. All three men were decapitated for defending their faith during the third century's persecution of the Church," Gaston Max said as he pointed out the sites as we walked.

"You missed your calling, *mon ami*," I said, laughing, but my companion continued as if he had not heard me.

"Today, Montmartre is the center of Parisian artistic life. Here, you will observe Bohemians and outcasts of every sort. Just as Van Gogh and Berlioz gravitated here in the past; one may now find Renoir, Monet, Modigliani, and countless other young talents mingling among the commoner and traveler alike."

"Did you memorize this from a brochure?" I asked.

Gaston Max smiled and glanced at the ground for a moment. "Are Englishmen not so proud of London?"

"It's not that at all, Max, but look around us. Do you see painters, composers, and mathematicians? I see undesirables and down and out derelicts, travelers, petty thieves, and vendors peddling illegal wares. This is the

Montmartre of today, if I am to judge by the evidence before my own eyes."

"Ah, they are but the sprinkling of Bohemian life, *mon ami*. We have a few more minutes to spare. Come, I will show you the *Lapin Agile*. That is truly the best that Paris has to offer."

Taking my arm in his, Gaston Max led me down the Rue des Saules past the Sacré-Coeur Basilica to the famous No. 22. If I was expecting more from this infamous cabaret, I was bound to be disappointed. It was a simple house decorated with a hand-painted sign of a rabbit jumping from a saucepan. Gaston Max turned to me as if he had read my mind.

"Do not let its quaint exterior fool you, the *Lapin Agile* was originally called the *Cabaret des Assassins*."

I was aghast. "Do you mean to tell me this house was a safe haven for Hashishins?"

Gaston Max smiled slyly and lowered his voice to a whisper.

"It still is a safe haven for Hashishins, *mon ami*, or what passes for them today. Anarchists and refugees from the Latin Quarter congregate here as much as the intellectuals who spend their days arguing the definition of Art. So watch your tongue and forget that you are with a member of the Sûreté. It wouldn't do to mention such things in Montmartre if you wish to leave with your throat intact."

A harsh winter wind blew upon our backs. Gaston Max hurriedly led the way to the Lodge of the Grand Orient of France. It was just after six o'clock. We stood on the steps with our heads down and our hands buried deep in our pockets.

"Good evening, gentlemen. I am sorry to have kept you waiting."

A man in a heavy overcoat and muffler had appeared, seemingly out of nowhere, on the steps next to us. I recognized Thomas Valley's soulless black eyes glowing like burning coals from under the wide brim of his hat.

"Come inside and out of the cold before you both catch your death of pneumonia."

He stepped up to the large double doors and produced a key from the chain around his waist. A few moments later, he held one of the large double doors open, inviting us within.

"Welcome to the Lodge of the Grand Orient of France, Dr. Petrie," Thomas Valley smiled, as Max and I followed him inside the large double doors.

I looked about the interior of the dimly lit Lodge. The familiar Masonic emblem of a compass and a square set against a pyramid inscribed with the letter *G* hung from banners behind the stone altar. We were completely alone in the room.

"How good of you to notice, Doctor. Freemasonry's roots can be traced back to the time of Ancient Egypt, Assyria, and Babylon," Valley spoke, as he climbed the steps to the altar. "The stonecutters of King Solomon's Temple are sacred to Freemasonry. First among them was Hiram Abiff who refused to reveal the secrets of his trade upon pain of death. You will find the Brotherhood of Magi is not so different from Freemasonry… in these respects."

I cleared my throat nervously. "You mentioned that Max and I needed to become Initiates before arranging our meeting with Esteban Milagro. You realize, of course, that neither of us are magicians by any definition of the word."

Thomas Valley laughed good-naturedly. "Of course, Dr. Petrie, of course. Nor are the majority of Initiates to Freemasonry actual masons. The names of both societies honor their origins, but their membership is happily not so restrictive in these modern times."

"Are the two societies associated with one another in some fashion?" Gaston Max asked.

Valley thought for a moment, then shrugged. "Not really, I suppose. There are, of course, members common to both societies. There are also some who would argue there is only one secret society in the entire world, but it chooses different identities to suit its many purposes. The truth is far from absolute. Long ago, I learned not to be troubled by such trivialities. The question now is simply whether you are both willing to accept my offer and become Initiates of the Brotherhood?"

I felt uneasy about being made an Initiate of this Order and suspected Gaston Max felt the same. I wondered what my father would have done had he found himself in similar circumstances. Perhaps he had, and it was merely one more facet of his life that had been kept hidden from me.

"I humbly accept your offer of membership. It is an honor to join your august ranks."

I was startled by the hollow echo of my own voice. I had not thought the words that I clearly heard myself say, and yet I had said them all the same. I was standing upon the stone steps of the altar with Gaston Max at my side. I felt as if I were watching a play unfold where an actor had assumed my role. Gaston Max nodded his assent and repeated the formal reply I had given. Valley smiled and placed his hands firmly on my shoulders and forced me to kneel down upon the stone altar.

"Behold your Worshipful Master."

I lowered my head before him. Thomas Valley then moved aside to stand in front of Gaston Max and likewise forced him to kneel and repeated the same words. He then returned to stand before me.

"Will you swear your allegiance before Jah-Bul-On, the Grand Magician who conjured this Universe and All Others; He Who May Not Be Known; He Who Is Boundless and Eternal; He Who Is the Intangible Maker of Worlds?"

I felt my nerve failing me. This was too pagan for my liking. How could I avoid this entrapment and still gain access to Esteban Milagro? Would lack of intent free me from being bound to my vow? Thomas Valley smiled in paternal amusement as if he suspected the anxiety I was feeling.

"Neither of you need fear responding," he said. "The Grand Magician is not a man, but rather Nature herself. It is the force and energy giving form to each stone and star. It is the spark of life in each man and beast upon the Earth. All existence is one so the myth of one true faith is rendered meaningless. Man's religions will rise and fall, but the Brotherhood of Magi is built on the solid rock of reason and not upon the shifting sands of superstition."

"I swear my allegiance," I replied.

Thomas Valley stepped aside and repeated the same oath to Gaston Max. He, too, swore his allegiance. Valley then returned to stand before me and, reaching into his pocket, withdrew a handkerchief and placed the blindfold over my eyes.

"This is the Hoodwink. You have been blinded by the false religions of man. You have been enslaved by the ignorance of man's science. You have repeated your father's errors and clothed your natural beauty in the pollution of man's profanity."

I listened as Valley stepped aside and the ritual was repeated for Gaston Max. Valley then returned to stand before me and I felt him place a rope about my neck.

"This is the Cable Tow. You have been bound against your will. Now you shall submit to the Will of Your Worshipful Master for only the Brotherhood of Magi may lead you out of the darkness and into the spiritual light. You have been immersed in tainted waters and seek to be baptized anew. You must choose one of the four canals to pass through before you may be purified. Shall it be *gutta, pectora, manus,* or *pedes*?"

As he said each word, I felt Valley run a dull blade along my throat, my chest, my hands, and my feet. He paused, waiting for me to choose.

"*Pedes*," I replied in a hoarse whisper, guessing what my choice would entail.

There was a pause of what felt like an eternity before I felt Valley grasp my leg, undo my shoe and remove it along with my sock. There was a sudden sensation, like a tickle, and then a sudden feeling of coldness that quickly gave way to the pain of extreme heat. I knew my foot had been slashed at the ankle. I bit my lip so as to maintain my composure.

I listened as he moved on and repeated the ritual to Gaston Max. I heard the hesitation in Gaston Max's voice as he made the same choice as I had taken. If the Frenchman was startled by what followed, he gave no audible sound.

Too soon for my liking, Thomas Valley stood before me once more and spoke.

"You must take care and be circumspect of what you eat and drink, what you say and think, what you do, and where you go. Do you most solemnly promise and swear to always hail, ever conceal, and never reveal any of the arts or the parts of the points of the hidden mysteries of the Brotherhood of Magi binding yourself under no less a penalty than that of having your throat cut, your tongue torn out, or your body buried in the rough sands of the sea?"

"I most solemnly promise and swear," I replied.

The same oath was then sworn by Gaston Max before Valley returned to stand before me once more.

"Rise and accept your place among the Brotherhood of Magi, Initiate Petrie." Thomas Valley's voice echoed through the empty hall.

I inclined my head and the rope was lifted from my neck and the blindfold removed from my eyes. I turned and watched as the same was done to Gaston Max. Thomas Valley moved to the center of the altar and stood at equal distance between us.

"Now that you are both Initiates and have pledged your allegiance to the Law, you may join me as my guests at the private party Esteban Milagro has arranged for seven o'clock this evening at the *Lapin Agile*. You will both need to know the password to gain entrance."

"And what is this password?" I asked.

Thomas Valley smiled. His unnaturally black eyes seemed to shine with forbidden knowledge.

"The password is *Bismillah*. In the name of God."

I stumbled backwards as if I had been struck. The password used by the Brotherhood of Magi was the very word that had precipitated Greba's murderous attempt on my life. It was the very word that once uttered had caused Thomas Valley to lose consciousness in Greba's hotel room. The very word I was instructed to intone when I was given that mysterious icon by what I believed to be Eltham's ghost. I felt sure that I was close to fitting the pieces of the puzzle together, but I was unable to focus my mind upon it as that dread word kept echoing in my head despite all my efforts to shut it out.

I felt a chill run down my spine. I had acted rashly, caring little for oaths made to an organization whose ideals meant nothing to me. I might as well have sworn my allegiance to the Si-Fan. Nayland Smith would have cursed me for a fool and rightly so.

"If there is a Grand Magician operating behind all of this, Petrie," I heard Smith's voice speaking to me in my head, "it is the insidious Dr. Fu Manchu."

"You're right, Smith," I thought, "and I foolishly walked directly into his trap."

## 16. NOM D'UN HOMME FATAL

The smell of Turkish cigarettes and opium filled the air as Gaston Max and I were permitted entrance to the private room at the *Lapin Agile* having separately supplied the password to the burly Arab who stood at the door. Thomas Valley's insistence on our joining the party a quarter of an hour late had aroused my suspicion. If we were truly Initiates to the Brotherhood of Magi and his guests at Esteban Milagro's private party, then why was it necessary to delay our arrival?

My eyes stung with the heavy smoke that permeated the room. I recognized none of the faces before me. Thomas Valley was certainly nowhere to be seen. Max and I had seated ourselves at a small wooden table in the corner of the room. The tabletop was covered in initials carved into the wood. A furtive glance at the neighboring tables told me that such is or at least was the custom at the *Lapin Agile*. We ordered our drinks and sat observing our surroundings.

"There is Monsieur Valley now," Gaston Max leaned over to speak in my ear as the waiter served us our drinks. Thomas Valley had entered the room with a party of six or seven Arabs. He had his arm around a heavy-set sheikh and was gesticulating wildly with his other hand as he spoke.

"Excuse me," I spoke to our waiter. "When is Señor Milagro expected to arrive?"

Gaston Max raised a hand to his forehead as if he were going to be ill.

The waiter looked at me under a furrowed brow. "I do not know who this Señor Milagro is. This is Prince Abard's private party."

He nodded toward the table nearest the stage where the sheikh had now seated himself along with Valley and several other Arabs.

"I've never heard of him. What is he prince of?" I asked.

Gaston Max snorted into his drink. The waiter smiled.

"He is a self-styled prince, but he claims to be in exile. Much more romantic, you see."

I thanked the waiter and handed him a generous tip for his trouble.

"You do realize you could have had us killed?" Gaston Max hissed at me over his Brandy. "Never appear ignorant of your host at a private party."

I was incredulous at the severity of his reprimand. "Didn't you hear the waiter just now? That's not…"

"I heard him and keep your voice down! Monsieur Valley tells us our host is Esteban Milagro. The waiter says it is this Prince Abard instead. Monsieur Valley was either mistaken or Señor Milagro is wearing a disguise. Since Monsieur Valley is sitting with Prince Abard, it is only logical to deduce the latter is the correct explanation."

"Why would Milagro need to disguise himself?" I whispered.

"Do not confuse the Lodge with the Brotherhood of Magi. They are separate and distinct entities. It is quite likely that Esteban Milagro is welcome to one and not the other. Hence the need for the disguise."

As if on cue, Prince Abard stood up at his table. All conversation in the room ceased as every eye turned toward the imposing figure of the rotund, but muscular Arab. He raised his hands and addressed all who were assembled as his guests.

"Thank you, *effendi*. May Allah grant each of you the reward you have earned this very night." He nodded his head to allow time for the thunderous applause of his guests to subside. "This evening, we have prepared a special entertainment for the benefit of a loyal friend who has come to us all the way from England."

The Arab gestured to where Thomas Valley sat. I studied his face closely and would have sworn the publisher looked more fearful than gracious upon hearing his host's generous remarks.

"He honors us with his presence here tonight. He is a friend to the Fellowship and seeks to bring us closer together with our separated Brethren."

At this last remark from Prince Abard, there was a murmur of dissension among the crowd. It was clear that such sentiments were not welcome. The Arab raised his hands to placate them.

"There are those who believe that we have become set in our ways for far too long. Old rivalries should be forgotten. Our common enemy should become our common goal to unite us as once we were united. Do such men speak wisdom or heresy? It is not for one as unworthy as me to judge."

He paused momentarily. I could not help but suspect his show of humility was intended to be ironic.

"Perhaps when you learn that tonight's tribute to our friend from across the Channel was arranged by the man who had once sworn to kill him, you will better appreciate that old animosities can be set aside and new bonds forged. Enough of this idle chatter. Let us eat and drink and love till at last our appetites are sated... for one evening at least."

There was another explosion of applause as the massive Arab resumed his seat. All eyes turned to the small wooden stage at the front of the room. A flimsy, smoke-stained curtain lifted jerkily to reveal Prince Abard's entertainment in Thomas Valley's honor. An Arab sat cross-legged upon a divan playing some sort of reed pipe. Every so often, he paused for breath, and would intone the following in a wavering, nasal voice:

"*Abu Jajouka... Akbar Pan... Muzzawie... Abu bin Jajouka... Akbar Ali Jajouka...*"

Finally, on the third of these vocal interludes, a figure emerged from behind the stage. A beautiful dancer, dressed in traditional Egyptian garb, climbed the few steps to the top of the wooden dais. At her appearance, the clientele in the *Lapin Agile* erupted with applause and barely-constrained enthusiasm. Max and I did our best to imitate their example.

Slim hips swayed to the eerie sound of the reed pipe as the dancer captivated the crowd. Her neck, breasts, and navel were adorned with strung beads and diaphanous silk that glistened as she trembled before the reed pipe's mesmerizing tune. Her face was covered in a veil, but the delicate bridge of her nose, the heavily-rouged cheekbones, and those magnificent dark eyes swathed in silver and gold left little doubt that beneath the veil lay a mouth promising a thousand delights.

What was visible of her face recalled my beloved Karamaneh, but happily that was the extent of the resemblance for the dancer was far from buxom. It mattered naught as her thin frame and delicate features more than made up for any deviation from Western notions of beauty. The pipe-playing ceased, and the cross-legged Arab intoned once more…

"*Abu Jajouka… Akbar Pan… Muzzawie… Abu bin Jajouka… Akbar Ali Jajouka…*"

The dancer bowed low as the music ceased and remained in that position while the pipe-player continued to intone in Arabic. As the last note died, the clientele began to beat a tattoo upon their tables. Slowly, the dancer straightened as her slim hips began to gyrate to the rhythm and increased in intensity as the tribal drumming upon the tables grew still more furious. Max and I joined in, quite genuinely this time, as the rhythmic pounding and the rapid movement of her hips was quite infectious.

As the breathtaking performance reached its climax, the dancer let out a high-pitched scream of ecstasy; I felt the blood rushing through my body in anticipation. She reached forward and tore the veil from her dusky face. I stared aghast as I recognized the face in the spotlight that had so enthralled me and every man in the *Lapin Agile* belonged to Karamaneh's brother, Aziz!

I was dumbstruck. Why would Aziz be party to such a bizarre and disturbing charade? How was this entertainment an appropriate tribute to Thomas Valley? I caught myself short. Enlightened as to the truth of the situation, I turned my attention from Aziz to Thomas Valley. The look upon his face was one of abject horror.

Perhaps I was wrong, I thought.

No, it dawned upon me, his horrified reaction was not because of Aziz; rather it was because of Prince Abard and his cronies. It was clear the other Arabs at the table were pressed close to prevent him from moving. He was trapped. What any of it meant, I could not guess. That it spelt trouble for Thomas Valley was patently obvious.

I was about to speak to Gaston Max when Aziz stepped down from the stage and sauntered over to Prince Abard's table. He stood before Thomas Valley and smiled wickedly. His teeth glittered eerily in the candlelight.

"His master sends his regrets that he cannot be here in person, but trusts that you will accept this gift in appreciation," Prince Abard spoke with mock politeness.

"Oh God, no!" Gaston Max murmured.

I was about to turn and ask him what the matter was when I saw Valley begin to struggle for freedom. The Arabs surrounding him held him firm. Prince Abard stood and moved behind Valley's chair. He grasped the publisher's head and roughly pushed him forward. Aziz leaned close and placed his arms about Thomas Valley's neck in an embrace. The boy's lips parted. His head tilted. His mouth moved along Valley's lips with a sudden jerking motion back and forth as Valley struggled to resist. Valley lolled back in his chair as if he were delirious. My mind reeled as I saw the crimson smear across his mouth spread rapidly down along the side of his left cheek.

"*Nom d'un petit bonhomme!*" Max cried. "He has been cut!"

It was true enough. The gleam in Aziz's smile had been a razor blade. Valley's mouth had been sliced from cheek to cheek. It was one of the most painful acts I have ever witnessed. The Arabs released their hold on the poor man. Thomas Valley collapsed to the floor, his face a bloody mockery of a smile.

"Quick! We must help him!" I hissed to Gaston Max.

The Frenchman held up a hand and slowly shook his head without glancing at me.

"*Non, mon ami.* We must proceed with the utmost caution if we are to avoid a similar fate. Monsieur Valley has been identified as a traitor. For all we know, it is because of his dealings with us tonight. Prince Abard said something about an enemy paying tribute to him and referred to the she-male being a gift from this same personage. We must find out who is this enemy of Monsieur Valley."

"It is Dr. Fu Manchu, I am sure of it," I hissed. "The boy is called Aziz. He has been enslaved by the Si-Fan in the past and must have fallen under their power again. Nayland Smith and I had liberated him once before, now we must do so again."

I started to rise, but Max roughly grabbed my shoulder and forced me down.

"You will do nothing of the sort. I am sorry for you. I realize it must have been difficult for you to have seen this. The world is filled with many kinds of people. There will always be those who seek to exploit that which makes even the strongest of men vulnerable. I speak of the uncontrollable inclinations of the human heart. A young woman or a young man may become a potent weapon with which to punish one's enemies. That is what this infernal Dr. Fu Manchu is doing here tonight to strike back at poor Monsieur Valley. There is nothing to be done for either of them now. If you were to speak with Aziz, you would only doom the both of you. It is better if we bide our time and try to depart separately. You made an unfortunate impression upon our waiter, but hopefully, in all of the excitement this evening, he will forget you, if only for a little while. That is all we need to make good our escape. Let us meet outside the Lodge of the Grand Orient of France on the Rue des Abbesses in say half an hour? I am going now. Wait a few moments if you can before you attempt to make a move on your own."

I watched as he rose and fought his way through the tiny club. Max disappeared in a wave of excited Arabs. I finished my drink and tried to still my nerves. Aziz's appearance and all that had followed rattled me badly. Gaston Max was quite right in all he had said about Aziz being exploited as a tool of the Si-Fan for the same was also true of Kara. Brother and sister were both victims of a cruel overlord who used their beauty as bait to ensnare others in his web. I felt my emotions getting the better of me and rose and made my way to the door. Happily, I left the *Lapin Agile* a few minutes later without incident.

## 17. COUP DU PÈRE FRANÇOIS

"Where is he?"

Gaston Max had still not appeared. I had been standing outside the Lodge of the Grand Orient of France for nearly an hour. It was nearly black outside and the crowds were already dwindling. The cold air blowing in from the Seine chilled me to the bone. Several figures were approaching from around the corner. I wondered if Gaston Max were among them.

A heavy-set, well-dressed man broke from the small crowd and stopped in front of me. He tipped his hat as he asked me in French if I knew the time. I shook my head that I could not help him and tried to move past him as he smelled strongly of alcohol and I had no time to waste with a common drunk. Unexpectedly, the Frenchman threw his hat into my face. Before I could react, a wire had been wrapped around my throat from behind! I was being garroted! I struggled as I realized the entire group had me surrounded.

I was pushed back and forth as hands dug deep into my pockets and my arms were pinned behind me. I was choking, but could make no sound. I couldn't breathe or speak. I was fighting for consciousness when a head was rammed into my abdomen and then quickly rose to butt me under the chin.

I gasped in pain as the hold on my throat and my arms was released and my jacket was pulled down to confine me more easily. The man's head then rammed into my face again and again. My last conscious thought was the realization that I had fallen victim to *Les Apaches*.

My senses were a dim echo in a black void for some time. The slightest disturbance was indistinguishable from the sound of water splashing beneath me. A flash of light streaked across my face before fading to blackness. I was forcing my eyes shut. I was not dead, but as full consciousness returned to me, I wished I were.

How many days had elapsed, I could not guess. I had never known such pain before. Every part of my body felt wrenched and broken. I had no sense of balance. Slowly, I realized I was suspended in mid-air. My arms and legs were manacled. A pool of black water lay some eight feet beneath me.

The slightest exertion sent me swaying. I had already been sick several times. The vomit clung to my lips and chin. I could taste its foul stench in my mouth. Where was I? It was then I heard a faint chattering that appeared to be growing louder, echoing more clearly with each passing second. It was the same chattering I heard that night outside my apartment in Paris when Greba tried to murder me in my bed. Paris? Could this still be Paris? There was no way for me to be certain.

As the chattering grew louder, I recognized it as Peko, Dr. Fu Manchu's marmoset. So, I was a prisoner of the Si-Fan once more! The little monkey was scattering along a wall outside of my limited range of vision. He sounded as if the fury of Hell itself were at his tail. The marmoset stopped for a moment when it caught sight of me and let loose a volley of ill-sounding invective as if it recalled my identity from our past encounters.

Just as quickly as the chattering started, it stopped again. I heard Peko clattering back the way he had come until the noise faded to nothingness. There was only the incessant splashing of the stagnant water below.

Presently, I began to hear the sound of footsteps growing closer. I could hear hushed voices speaking, but I could not make out any words or even determine whether it was male or female voices engaged in conversation. The footsteps and voices ceased and, after an agonizing moment of straining to listen, a light appeared at the far end of the damp cellar and the sound resumed. It was growing closer with each passing second. Only then was I able to discern the footsteps were interspersed with a short dragging sound and then I knew!

Dr. Fu Manchu was approaching!

I strained my neck and tried to ignore the pain in my head. I could see him. He was flanked by several black-robed dacoits. Crimson bandanas tied round their heads, these deadly servants of the Si-Fan were convinced each victim whose life they claimed brought them one step closer to Paradise. The thought of the Devil Doctor commanding an army of these religious fanatics sent a shiver down my spine.

Dr. Fu Manchu's leg was still crippled from his stroke and he relied on the thick wooden walking stick to support his weight as he shuffled along the floor of the cellar. Any other man of his advanced age and fragile condition would have appeared frail and weak, but not him! That tall, thin frame still appeared strong despite his infirmity. Though stooped with age and ill health, his head was held high affording him full view of my predicament.

What pride he possessed! If ever a man deserved to indulge in that sin, it was the mind that housed that titanic intellect. A barely perceptible layer of fine, white hair outlined his skull. I have never lost my fascination for that amazing face, so lined with wrinkles that a grown man could trace a path through its maze with two burly fingers held side to side. But that was still not his most striking feature. As it had always been, it was his eyes that held me rapt. Those fabulous cat-green eyes that sparkled like jade lit by some unearthly luminescence. It was impossible to think of anyone or anything but him when one stood in the presence of the magnificent Dr. Fu Manchu.

"Good evening, Dr. Petrie," he hissed in that alternately guttural and sibilant whisper that characterized his speech. "We meet again... in Paris, no less. Your continued survival is rivaled only by your dogged determination to force my hand where you are concerned. It pains me, but I must finally be rid of you once and for all."

So I had learned that I was still in Paris, at least.

"Who is forcing your hand?" I spoke as best as I was able. "You abducted me... tortured me... now, you claim that it was I who has forced you to act. If you really possess even a shred of the honor you boast of, you will set me free. I have done you no wrong."

Those few short sentences left me exhausted. My head sagged under the strain.

"I fear you are incorrect on all counts, Doctor." Fu Manchu's eyes clouded over in that peculiar birdlike fashion whenever he became emotional. "I did not seek to abduct you, nor did I intend for you to suffer in these medieval surroundings, and yes, Dr. Petrie, you have wronged me many times over, not in the least by compromising one of my servants. No, you have brought this fate upon yourself with your useless blundering. I have merely intervened to ensure you receive an honorable death."

He quivered for a moment and then his eyes reverted to their natural state.

"I have much work to do. I bid farewell to you. If you possess the intelligence that once I credited you with, then you will appreciate the circumstances of your impending demise. I regret that I will be unable to attend to you any longer as I must prepare for my return to your beloved England once my business here is concluded."

I thought, for a passing moment, that I detected a hint of amusement on those saturnine features as he turned and signaled to his dacoits that it was time to leave. Peko came chattering and scampering to greet him as if the marmoset had merely waited for our conversation to conclude. The little beast sprung to his shoulder and dug its claws into the thick golden robe that regaled the Devil Doctor. I could hear him whispering to his simian pet and then pausing to allow time for the creature to reply as if they understood one another's language. They continued on that way until their footsteps and the sound of that maddening conversation receded in the distance.

I let my head sink down once more. It was hopeless. I was beaten. Gaston Max had been delayed and now there would be no way for him to pick up my trail. I was too bruised and battered to make any effort to save myself. I had come this far to try to prevent more needless deaths only to die myself. Such was the risk I had been willing to take, but I never expected to die alone.

I thought of Eltham and all he had wrought. There were some, Nayland Smith among them, who suggested the blame for the Boxer Uprising could be laid at the feet of over-zealous, intolerant missionaries such as Eltham. The Boxer Uprising had seen thousands of innocent Chinese and white men and women slaughtered. It had brought the mighty armies of England, Europe, and the colonies together to unite against a common enemy. The Boxer Uprising had doomed the once-noble Manchu dynasty to extinction. It had brought the terror of Fu Manchu upon the British Empire. Ironically, the very ideals Eltham embraced that had caused this ceaseless turmoil were rejected by him in his last days. Nevertheless, the Boxer Uprising could be said to have claimed Eltham's life just as it had thousands of others. It was justice, in a way, but still the repercussions were being felt. I thought of Greba and Thomas Valley and winced in pain. Too much blood had been spilt. I wanted to hide away and never see another day dawn again.

"Darling, oh my poor darling!"

I struggled to lift my head as I recognized the musical tinkle of the voice of my beloved Karamaneh.

"Hush, dearest, don't try to move or speak."

My sweat-stung eyes tried to focus on her smooth, dusky skin. Karamaneh had come to rescue me! Had she stolen a key? Had she slit Fu Manchu's throat whilst he slept or put a bullet in his heart? She must have guessed my thoughts for she sadly shook her head.

"No, darling. There is no escape for you this time. I have prayed that Allah grant you a swift and merciful death for I can do nothing to help you. I am here only because he allowed me to see you one last time. I do not wish to be present for... for what is to come, but he granted me the favor of saying goodbye."

She was on the shore and I was suspended above a pool of filthy water. I would never again know the touch of those soft, warm lips on mine. I could see the tears coursing her cheek. She made no attempt to hide them.

"We return to London presently. I shall always love you. My heart shall belong to none other than my brave and foolish..."

Kara hung her head and sobbed. Emotion had choked my name in her throat. She was condemned to live out her days in the household of Dr. Fu Manchu with no hope of liberation. There was no chance now of our being reunited or wed. We would never live happily ever after as we both so desperately wanted. Love is a childish dream, but it was one we believed could be made real in our case. Life is filled with many paths left untaken. This was but one.

"If Allah is willing we will see one another again in Paradise." Her voice was but a whisper that barely carried to my ears.

I shut my eyes to block out her words. I did not now nor had I ever believed in a life after death. Kara was but a child in so many ways, yet I had loved her like no other woman I have ever known. I kept my eyes sealed until I was sure that she was gone.

## 18. IN THE BELLY OF THE BEAST

The hours passed slowly, but I felt no hunger or thirst or want of sleep. My only wish was for it to be over with once and for all. No more suffering, only blackness. I wanted it finished. It came sooner than I expected.

Footsteps echoed along the walls once more. I no longer felt fearful. My visitors this time were white men dressed in bowlers and topcoats. *Les Apaches!* They stopped and parted to allow space for one of their number to step forward. It was not an Apache, but rather the Arab sheikh from the *Lapin Agile*.

"Prince Abard!"

The fat Arab smiled. His massive belly rolled as a low chuckle reverberated around the dank cellar.

"You know me. How nice. But I do not know you."

I gritted my teeth as I tried to find the strength to speak. "Ask Fu Manchu…"

The Arab's eyes widened before disappearing into the fat folds of skin that sagged around his cheeks.

"Oh! We know Dr. Fu Manchu, do we? Well! Now I begin to understand why the good doctor demands such special treatment for you."

The laughter stopped instantly as his face darkened in anger.

"Idiot! Infidel! Dog of a Nazarene! You could not stay silent! You had to attract his attention! See where it gets you? Bah, the worst is yet to come."

His anger passed as quickly as it had risen and he broke into hearty gales of laughter once more. What value did his threats hold? I had already accepted the fact I would meet my death this day. There was nothing to fear beyond this point. My only regret was that I would not have a chance to say goodbye to Nayland or to hold Kara in my arms one last time.

"Prince Abard, tell me... the Si-Fan, the Brotherhood of Magi... how are they connected?"

His eyes widened once more and he laughed harder still, stamping a massive tree trunk of a leg while he chortled. I was struggling to stay conscious. Was this death? I did not want to die with questions left unanswered.

"Fulton Denison..." I groaned. "Esteban Milagro, are you who they say?"

The fat Arab threw back his head and roared even harder. If Gaston Max was correct and this was Esteban Milagro in disguise, he certainly made no sign to indicate it were so.

"Neville McBride... Trelawney..." I heard my voice rise. "Ursula Trelawney..."

"Silence!" the Arab screamed at me. "Do not dare to question me further!"

His outburst roused me enough to regain control of my failing senses. There was life in me yet.

"You want me to explain it all to you before you die? Is that it, Englishman?"

He spat upon the ground and uttered a vile curse.

"Why would I do that, eh?" he yelled. "Why would I give you the peace of mind? I would rather you die wondering. Go to the Thousand Hells dreaming of what you could have done with the knowledge. Nothing! That is what you could have done with it. Nothing! You are still going to die!"

He was right. I thought about my predicament and actually smiled. That old adage about it being easier to smile than frown is a lie. Smiling hurt far worse, I am sure of it.

"I will give you something to chew on while you're in the belly of the beast, Englishman." He laughed wickedly and again spat upon the ground. "It is all for the Seal of Solomon. That is the key. Not the Si-Fan. Not the Brotherhood of Magi. Not nobody or nothing. All that matters is the Seal. It is the prize to be cherished above all other treasures. It is worth the price of this entire world."

He laughed uproariously and turned his back on me. He pushed his way through the small group of *Apaches* and waved them to follow him.

I was alone again with naught but the sound of water collecting in the foul-smelling pool beneath me.

I think I actually slept as my brain had ceased to function for a time. I was suddenly aware of movement and sound whereas before there was only nothingness. A terrible clanging and wrenching assaulted my senses. I was sick again. This time it was worse than before, I felt it rise from my bowels and fight its way, burning all the while, out of my throat.

Why were they pulling me? I was definitely aware of chains clattering and iron screeching. Was I being reeled into shore? Would I be lowered and allowed to feel the ground beneath my feet one more time before I died?

No, slowly I realized the wrenching and pulling was not the sound of the beam that supported my weight being moved; rather it was the sound and movement of a second beam being hoisted to join me. I turned my head for a better look and gasped.

I was no longer alone.

An iron cage had been pulled into the air and was inching its way closer to me with each passing minute.

Within the cage I saw three sets of wild, frightened eyes staring at me.

Good Lord! They were children!

The cage was now close enough for me to touch had my limbs not been manacled to the suspended beam. I could see them clearly. A fair-haired girl of no more than twelve, a young boy of seven or so, and a waif who looked to be four or five years old clung to the bars of the cage. They looked half-mad with starvation.

"Are you English?" a soft voice spoke.

"Yes…I am," I struggled to reply.

They just stared at me, not saying another word.

"You sound English, too," I rasped. "How… how did you come to be in Paris?"

"Paris? We're in Paris?"

The older girl's voice betrayed amazement, but the two smaller children had started to quietly sob at my words. She was a pretty little waif with golden tresses framing elfin features. Freckles dotted her face. A birthmark, so faint as to appear an embellishment, graced her cheek. One of her soft blue eyes contained a spot of brown adding further character to her already striking features. Under more pleasant circumstances, it was apparent she would have proven quite the charmer. She would not live to charm anyone now.

"Your Mummy… your Mummy must be frightfully worried about you," I said. "Don't you worry one bit. I'll see you home safely."

I didn't know if all three children were actually siblings and I knew I was lying through my teeth, but I believed it to be the only conscionable action to take under the circumstances.

"You'll see them home safely if their mother is a crocodile, otherwise... well... I'm afraid you've been telling pork pies to these dear, sweet children."

I twisted my neck so I could see Prince Abard and *Les Apaches* standing below us on the shore. He reached a staff up and prodded the cage roughly, sending it swaying in the process. The cage struck against my suspended beam and sent me swinging back and forth, smacking against the bars of their cage over and over again. The children were thrown to the floor of the cage and slid roughly against the sides.

"See?" he yelled. "See her yellow eyes through the portcullis? That's Mummy waiting for her babies."

I didn't know what he was talking about. Was he mad? I looked to where he pointed and then I saw it.

Great God in Heaven, I saw it.

An iron portcullis hung suspended from the roof of the cellar all the way down beneath the water. There, at the waterline, were two malevolent yellow eyes staring up at us. Never blinking, just staring. Yellow eyes that patiently waited for the portcullis to rise. Yellow eyes that patiently waited for the four of us to drop into the black waters below so it could feast.

What had the fat Arab said? Something for me to chew on in the belly of the beast. He had the unmitigated gall to call that abomination their Mummy. He would die this day. I would kill him. I didn't know how, but I would find a way. No man that evil deserved to live. He would die by my hands. I wanted it to be so. I wanted to kill him more than I wanted revenge on *Les Apaches.* I wanted to kill him more than I wanted to end the menace of Fu Manchu. I had made the decision to place my life in jeopardy and I fully understood the risks being taken. What had these children done to deserve to share my fate?

"Now is the time for you to make your choice, Englishman," he shouted. "It is Fu Manchu's parting gift to you."

Using all of his massive girth, Prince Abard pulled the heavy wooden lever that rose six feet in the air down towards the ground. Again the terrible wrenching and grinding of metal could be heard, but this time, it was the iron portcullis that was rising barely a few inches above the waterline. Slowly, those terrible yellow eyes drifted forward until they were directly underneath me.

"You have been granted the right of dealing death, Englishman. Who shall die first? Should I release you into the waters and let the children listen to the chomping and gnashing of the beast's teeth? Shall they hear your terrified screams for mercy or should they be released first instead? There are three of them. Perhaps one may drown or another's heart may burst before the crocodile finishes with the first of them. Who do you think it will desire the most, the big girl or the little one... or do you think she'll find the little boy to be the tastiest morsel instead?"

Prince Abard laughed wickedly.

I pushed myself sideways and hooked a manacled hand and foot through the bars of the children's cage.

"What have these children done to deserve this?" my broken voice shrieked.

"What have they done?" the Arab shouted back at me. "They stuck their noses where it didn't belong, just like you. They wouldn't stop their dirty little tongues from wagging. Stupid meddlers... they'll pay the price. They die first!"

"No!" I screamed in vain.

The Arab pulled a second wooden lever. There was a clanking of iron. The cage began to sway violently. I looked down as I heard the floor of the cage beginning to creak.

"Listen to me! Hang onto the bars!"

My own grip was far from sure. I was weakened and the manacles prevented me from grasping the bars of their cage properly. The three children did as I commanded and held onto the bars tightly, wrapping their legs around the lowest rungs.

I stared at them. The little brown-haired boy was closest to me. He looked thin and a bit sickly with dark rings under both his eyes. The dark-haired waif next to him must have been his little sister as the resemblance between the two was strong. Brown curls dangled in front of terrified eyes. The older fair-haired girl gritted her teeth and refused to look at me.

The floor of the cage let go with a terrible clanging of metal. We watched it splash into the murky waters eight feet below us. There was a terrible splashing as the crocodile wrestled its way onto the cage floor, pushing it deeper below the water. Monstrous head raised defiantly, the mighty jaws of the beast snapped viciously at the air above as if willing the children to fall into its waiting mouth.

They were screaming. I hadn't heard them at first, but all three of them were screaming in abject fear. I bit through my lower lip as I tried to cling to the side of their cage. There was more clanging. I could not tell if it was coming from above us or if it was the sound of the hungry crocodile struggling on the floating floor of the cage just a few feet below.

There was an unexpected feeling of weightlessness. I grasped the bars of their cage tightly with both my hands and feet. A rushing sound filled the air as I was crushed against the side of the cage.

Christ! God! Don't let me fall.

My face was smashed between the bars. My jaw pressed against the fingers of one of the children's hands. There was a terrible splash and all four of us were soaked with that foul brackish water. A hideous sound that could only have emanated from the throat of that dreadful creature ripped through the air. It was then I realized what had occurred.

The beam that had held me suspended had fallen from the ceiling of the cellar. Prince Abard had released my hold intending to send me into the water below.

The manacles! What had happened to my manacles? Why wasn't I dead?

I fought to turn my head slightly and I saw the broken rungs of the manacle upon my wrist. As I concentrated, I could feel them on both my wrists and my ankles. They must have snapped when the beam dropped. I recalled then the pain of my suspending beam scraping against my spine, pinning me to the side of the children's cage. My hold on the bars had been strong enough to tip the weight of the beam against my back and break its fall, if only momentarily. The manacles had snapped free against its weight and sent the beam plunging into the water below. I shook my head as I realized how close to unconsciousness the pain and my fear had brought me.

"I'm going to fall!"

It was the little girl's frantic plea that brought me round again. I couldn't see her, but I saw the older girl turning and looking at her, trembling.

"Oh God, no! Anna, hang on!" the fair-haired girl yelled.

*Do something!* I thought. *Do something. What could I do?*

There were only seconds to spare, that much was certain. My fingers did not want to let go, but I forced myself to scale down the rungs of the cage. As I reached the bottom, I realized my legs were dangling too close to the water. There was a terrible snapping sound and I winced in pain as the crocodile sprung into the air. I could feel the blood and the chill cavernous air on my exposed heel. The beast had only grazed me, but the injured heel was bleeding badly.

*Move your legs now before it's too late!*

I swung my legs up inside the now bottomless cage and struggled to bring an arm underneath to grasp a bar of the cage from the inside. I felt the rush of movement and heard the snap of the crocodile's jaws a second time, but this time it missed me. I swung myself under and up as the water splashed below. I chanced a quick glance beneath me and saw blood washing over the creature's back.

Could all of that blood be from my foot? I wondered for a moment. No, the beast must have been cut by the suspension beam when it dropped upon its back. I smiled grimly, invigorated by the thought that monstrosity had been injured.

I climbed up inside the cage rapidly. Using my bare feet as a second pair of hands, I locked my toes around the bars as I climbed. I reached the little girl and climbed up and around her, pressing her tight against the cage with my torso.

"I have you. I have you," I repeated.

The clanging of metal resounded again and the cage swung violently. Prince Abard was struggling with the wooden lever to release the cage! There was only one hope.

"Climb!" I yelled. "Climb to the top of the cage!"

I grabbed the waif with one arm and climbed as rapidly as I could manage using my free arm and my feet. The boy half-climbed and half-clung to my side. The older girl did as I asked and climbed with every ounce of youthful strength she could muster and quickly outdistanced me.

A shot rang out!

Good God! No! Not the children!

I glanced down to the ground and saw the fat Arab lying slumped over the wooden lever. His neck was twisted crookedly. Blood was running down his face from a blackened hole in his forehead. A volley of gunshots followed. *Les Apaches* were being cut down before they had a chance to react. I saw gendarmes spill out over the shore and there was Gaston Max leading the charge!

"Docteur Petrie!" he cried. "Hold on, *mon ami*!"

Gaston Max! I had never been so happy to see a man before! Suddenly, there was a terrible row and scuffle as Max and the gendarmes backed away in fright. It was then that I saw it! The crocodile had abandoned us and was wading quickly onto the shore in the direction of prey that were within easy reach.

Shoot! Why didn't they shoot?

The creature's awful jaws snapped rapidly. A low moan creaked from its throat, and then it turned unexpectedly and sprung upon the body of the dead Arab slumped over the wooden lever.

Oh God!

I watched as the Arab's head disappeared into the mouth of the crocodile. Bullets rang out. The crocodile collapsed on top of the Arab's dead body. I heard the clank of the metal and felt the cage begin to sway before I realized what was happening. The crocodile's weight had released the jammed lever beneath Prince Abard's now headless corpse.

"Don't let go!" I gasped.

The children screamed. The cage rocked violently. Iron cranked and bent. I held the little waif tight and grabbed onto the boy's arm, twisting it furiously to keep him pressed against the bars as the swaying cage plunged sidelong to the ground below.

There was a terrible rushing of wind, and then it was over. We were thrown sideways across the bars as water splashed onto us. We coughed and sputtered as we scrambled out of the cage, crawling in the opposite direction where once we would have been forced to climb. One of the spikes at the bottom of the cage had pierced through the crocodile's back and skewered the beast and the dead Arab into the ground.

"Don't look!" I covered the two littlest children's eyes.

The older girl shook her head and grimaced. "No. I want to see."

I handed the two smaller children into the arms of the waiting gendarmes and herded the older girl out in front of me.

"Max!" I yelled. Tears were streaming down my cheeks as I embraced the Frenchman. "Thank you! God! Thank you!"

He smacked me hard upon the back, laughing. "There is no need to thank me, *mon ami*. I am only doing what I am paid to do."

"Where are we anyway?" I exclaimed.

"At the base of Montmartre. Underground. You should have listened more closely to my history lesson."

The Frenchman smiled.

At the Sûreté, arrangements were made for the safe return home of the three children to England. A gendarme gathered information to wire their families.

The older girl, Alexandra, explained she and her two younger friends, Michael and his sister, Anna, had been abducted from outside their homes in Dartford. Instantly, I understood why the children had been taken. These were the same three neighborhood children who had discovered the six snowmen outside the McBride residence. Their lives would be forever tainted with the knowledge that this world is far more evil and dangerous than most men ever fathom. I pitied them as I pitied all victims of the Si-Fan who survived. There was nothing more to be done except to let them try to resume living normal lives. For me and Gaston Max, the battle waged on.

## 19. THE DEVIL YOU KNOW

I awoke to a Paris of nightmares. I was trapped in a city where none could be trusted. I was seeking a phantom hidden in shadow-shrouded cellars protected by those who swore allegiance to the Si-Fan and its mission to topple the British Empire. I was seeking a madman who walked the same path as the degenerate students of occult knowledge who called themselves the Brotherhood of Magi. Everywhere I went, anyone might have reason to suppress information, thwart my efforts, or snuff out my life. I pressed my fist against my teeth to stop myself from sobbing. I felt like a child, but I wanted nothing more than to be back in London and let the burden of responsibility rest squarely upon Nayland Smith's more capable shoulders.

I bathed and dressed and quietly checked out of the hotel. I had barely slept the night before for fear of assassins and in the unsettling knowledge that I and the Sûreté's most celebrated detective had sworn our allegiance to a murderous secret society. I did not wish to spend another night in a hotel where men such as he knew I resided.

I called at the hospital to check on Greba. Dr. Marat was not on duty, but the nurse led me to Greba's private room. She was sitting up in bed when I arrived. She looked pale and drawn. As I entered the room, I was disturbed to see her lips moving as if she were in conversation with an imaginary companion.

"Hello, Greba." I said softly.

For a moment, she ignored me. Her lips ceased moving and I realized she must have been praying. Her head dropped back on the pillow and her eyes shut.

"I was hoping I would never see you again."

I struggled to find words to reply as she turned and stared at me.

"They told me how I was injured. I can't believe this is real. I must have gone mad after learning what had happened to Father."

So great was my regret for having taken advantage of her moment of weakness, it did not cross my mind that the guilt she bore was for her attempt on my life and not our night together. Relieved, I moved a chair over to the bed and sat beside her.

"It's a beautiful morning, Greba. The night is over and the sun returns to herald the start of a new day. You must understand that you are not to blame for your actions."

She buried her face in her hands. I reached out to comfort her.

"My darling, you must believe me. Your mind was not your own. You had fallen under the influence of Dr. Fu Manchu."

She gasped as she looked up at me.

"Will it never end? Will I never be free of him? Wasn't Father's life enough of a price to pay? Why can't he leave me be?"

I knelt on the edge of the bed and took her in my arms. I wanted nothing more than to comfort her as I gently stroked her hair.

"It's all right, Greba. Let's leave this place. Let's go home."

She choked back tears upon hearing my words.

"Home? I have no home to go to. Where would I be safe? Where could I go where I would escape his notice? He's haunted me for years. He drove Father from his faith and into the madness of Fulton Denison and his parasitic followers."

Fulton Denison! In all that had happened recently, I had completely forgotten that name. Thomas Valley claimed that this was the man who had introduced Neville McBride to Reverend Eltham. This surely pointed to some connection with the Brotherhood of Magi and quite possibly with the Si-Fan as well. Here was another piece of the puzzle that would have to be found before all would become clear to us.

"Never mind that now, Greba. Let's first get back to London. We'll let Nayland Smith sort out the rest of it."

For the first time since I had arrived, I saw a glimmer of Greba's old self once more. "Mr. Smith, of course. How could I have forgotten him? Oh, Dr. Petrie, can you do it? Can you really get us back to England?"

I was thrown by the formality with which she addressed me. The post-hypnotic effect must have robbed her of the memory of what had happened the night before she tried to kill me.

"Yes, my darling. I shall get us safely back to England. It's the least I can do," I replied quietly.

I went into the hall and asked the duty nurse to hail me a cab. Greba was hurriedly dressing in the restroom. When she emerged, I noted her cheeks were flushed and her hands were trembling. I had made no plans on how to deal with the reaction her premature departure would precipitate. We were far too many floors up from the ground to make an exit by window feasible even had Greba not been shaking like a leaf.

A few minutes later, there was a knock upon the door and the duty nurse announced that my cab was ready. My face must have betrayed my nervousness for Greba's features suddenly drained of all color. We were being foolish in thinking our departure would be so simple. Her fragile condition and her criminal behavior made her a prisoner. This time there would be no easy escape.

"Trust me, Greba," I said, feeling not at all confident of our success. "Just follow my lead and we will be fine."

Her eyes searched mine for something to believe in. There was nothing for us to do but act. I knew myself well enough to know that I would not hold up long under scrutiny. I rose from the chair and folded my coat over one arm. I took Greba's arm and opened the door. We stopped in the doorway. I turned back toward her empty hospital bed, making sure that I was obscuring the duty nurse's view of Greba's face in the process.

"Take care, Greba, my dear. We will see you again soon."

I tipped my hat to the nurse as we made our way to the stairwell. For her part, Greba played the role perfectly as she looked straight ahead and walked with her arm linked in mine.

"Good day to you, Docteur Petrie. Good day, Mademoiselle," the duty nurse mumbled, failing to look up from her paperwork. If all went well, we would be at the station before our deception was discovered.

The cold morning air hit my cheek like the slap of a spurned lover. Greba bent like a willow against the fierce winter wind. I spotted the cab waiting for us at the curb. We walked toward the waiting automobile and paused, expecting the driver to emerge. The seconds ticked by. The wind and the cold and my fear of being apprehended won out over my patience. I held Greba tight as I reached for the back door of the cab and ushered her quickly inside. As I slammed the door shut behind me, I reached forward and grasped the driver roughly by the shoulder.

"You might have opened the door for us in this beastly weather," I snapped.

As he put the cab in gear, the driver turned back and leered at me. I fell back in my seat in a state of shock. The chalk white face... the hideously twisted grin... it was the burned Chinaman I had seen the night Eltham's ghost gave me that Eastern icon and taught me the Arabic word, *Bismillah*.

"Good God! Kau!" I gasped recalling the name Eltham had used.

That awful face bobbed menacingly. I realized that deformed leer was nearly identical to Thomas Valley's own scarred mouth. Suddenly, the truth dawned upon me. The Chinaman Kau had been punished by the Si-Fan in the same awful manner as Thomas Valley.

*Oh God in Heaven! We are taken. We are prisoners of Fu Manchu!*

There would be no escape for us a second time. I turned and reached for the door latch only to discover there was none on either side of the cab. We were trapped! Greba swooned and collapsed in my arms. I was helpless and drifting into a madness that threatened to devour every last shred of my sanity.

## 20. INTO THE SPHERE OF THE INFINITE

I was being driven in a speeding cab down the Champs-Elysées. Greba Eltham was slumped over next to me with her unconscious head resting in my lap. The past three weeks had seen me embroiled in constant intrigue with members of either the Si-Fan or the Brotherhood of Magi. It was clear that these two secret societies were either working against one another or in league. Now, I had been abducted and felt certain that my good fortune had finally played itself out.

There was no question that death was near at hand. It was this sense of desperation that led me to act rashly like a cornered beast. I rolled Greba's unconscious form off the seat of the cab and gently lowered her to the floor. I reached into my breast pocket and removed the icon of the encircled star that I had received the night I first set eyes on Kau.

"*Bismillah.*"

I spoke the word through gritted teeth and repeated it as if a mantra until I found I was saying it without thinking. I reached forward into the front of the cab. Kau turned his head momentarily and I lashed out. The point of the encircled star scored a cut just below his right eye. I used the icon to gouge again and again into the side of his cheek as many times as I could. I kept repeating, "*Bismillah, Bismillah, Bismillah…*"

Kau reached out with his right arm and locked his fingers around my neck. He pulled me forward with a sudden wrench. The cab careened wildly on the icy road.

The disfigured Chinaman lunged forward on the brake and I found myself flung over the front seat. I had just enough time to move my free arm in front of my face as I smashed through the cab's windscreen.

I was in shock and could not yet feel any pain. Cold air assaulted me as the cab's bonnet dented beneath my weight. I bounced roughly and tumbled sideways off the bonnet of the car and onto the pavement. The cab screeched to a halt a few feet ahead of me. I was keenly aware of a throbbing pain now that I had landed on solid ground. Miraculously, nothing felt broken.

"*Bismillah, Bismillah, Bismillah…*"

The word was still pounding in my skull as I stumbled to my feet and staggered haphazardly up the steps in front of me. My vision was blurred. I was aware my head was bleeding. I couldn't let myself be recaptured by the Si-Fan and, now that I had aided Greba in escaping from the hospital, I had to avoid the authorities at all cost as well. There was nothing I could do for Greba now. There was nothing for me to do but to keep running.

I wiped my eyes clear of the blood and perspiration that stung them and pushed wide the great doors that opened on a most unexpected sight. The Bibliothèque Nationale held the libraries of every King of France dating back to the reign of Charles V. A veritable treasure trove of rare photographs, prints, coins, and priceless books were held under the huge gold-bedecked archway before me.

Libraries are the gateways to other worlds, my father often said. I hoped he was correct as I certainly needed to transport myself elsewhere immediately. My head was swimming. I made my way to the end of the great hallway and began the long climb up the winding marble staircase. The tapestries that hung upon the walls were truly breathtaking. Each floor was covered in riches. I thrilled to the sight and smell of those timeless treasures, aisle upon aisle, and floor upon floor. I could easily have lost myself for days within its walls.

I dabbed at my forehead and felt the blood drying. I was sore, but able to walk without too much pain. My luck had held out after all. I was fortunate to be in one piece after what had happened. At random, I selected a floor to stop at and lose myself within. I moved quickly down the aisle and disappeared between long rows of books. I hoped to impress any prying eyes as naught but an avid bibliophile hunting some musty old tome otherwise lost to the dim echoes of the forgotten past. Whilst busy acting out my role, a title at the bottom of the shelf caught my eye and I bent down to reach for the book.

"Is there anything in particular you are looking for, Monsieur?" A husky, yet delightfully feminine voice asked in French.

I looked up into the walnut-colored eyes of one of the most exquisite faces I have ever beheld. I straightened up before this perfect specimen of Gallic beauty. My face flushed as I savored her winsome smile, thick blond hair, and that intoxicating aura of attraction that only youth can convey with a complete absence of guile or effort.

"Excuse me?" I stammered.

"Oh, you are bleeding!" She switched to English. The slight hint of concern in that charming accent warmed my heart.

"I'm fine, really, just a... just a small accident. It looks far worse than it is, I assure you."

The French girl stared at my head injury for a moment, clearly unconvinced, but she was young enough not to make trouble, fortunately.

"My name is Michelle." She cleared her throat, nervously. "I am in charge of the occult collection. Is there anything in particular that Monsieur is looking for?"

A sudden inspiration seized upon me and I acted instantly.

"As a matter of fact, yes, there is. Do you have any titles published by a small English occult specialty press called McBride & Valley?"

I realized I must have sounded and looked more than a bit deranged. She smiled, doubtless accustomed to grown men making complete asses of themselves in her presence.

"*Oui, Monsieur.* As I said, this is the occult collection. We have one of their titles right here."

To my utter astonishment, she bent down, and pulled from the bottom shelf the very book that had caught my eye just a moment before. She handed it to me and I opened the book to the title page.

"*Into the Sphere of the Infinite.*" I read the words aloud as if transfixed. "*Translated and with a new Foreword by Ursula Trelawney from the original Spanish text by Esteban Milagro. 1912. McBride & Valley, publishers.*"

I quickly paged through the book. The frontispiece was a painting of a pale, featureless ghoul dressed in some sort of bright purple tunic. The ghoul's posture suggested he was dancing in some sort of Pagan ritual. The script below the photograph gave the author's year of birth and death as 1656 and 1717, respectively!

Esteban Milagro died nearly two centuries ago? Perhaps I was chasing ghosts after all.

"Can you tell me anything about this author?" I demanded snapping the book shut.

Michelle lifted her eyes heavenward and held up a forefinger as if to silence me.

"Esteban Milagro was a Spaniard burned at the stake for witchcraft in the 18th Century. He was the author of a notorious book of sorcery called *En el Esfera de la Infinito*, the English translation of which you are now holding. It was banned by the Church and suppressed for over a century. It was rescued from obscurity when a translation by the English magician, Ursula Trelawney, appeared just last year. Have you heard of her? I think she is sensational. It is said Mistress Trelawney constitutes the one serious rival to Aleister Crowley himself!"

I was aware my head had begun to bleed again. I dabbed at it nervously with my handkerchief.

"Why, yes. As it happens, I am familiar with the lady in question. I've even had the pleasure of seeing her in the flesh, so to speak."

Michelle stared at my head with some concern, so I hurriedly thanked her for her help and turned to immerse myself in the book in front of me. I paged through it initially as a distraction whilst waiting for the pretty young librarian to wander off and leave me in peace. As I did so, I quickly became engrossed in what I saw. The first few pages were the usual rubbish occult history, but then I stumbled upon a series of line drawings of a sacrificial altar. To my shock and amazement, I realized I had seen these same drawings before in the box I uncovered in Kane Keller's apartment! Here was the final proof, if any were needed, that Keenan Pethig had been murdered by occultists. The poisoned pork... my mind turned again to the warning in my dream of the goddess Isis and her father:

*Avoid that which is unclean*, Fu Manchu had said. I had heard a similar warning since then... but where?

I had it! When Gaston Max and I were blindfolded in the Lodge of the Grand Orient of France, Thomas Valley had warned us to take care and be circumspect of what we eat and drink, what we say and think, what we do, and where we go.

Great Scott! Was I really going mad or did this all actually point to some larger truth hidden in the conspiratorial workings of the world's great secret societies? Did they actually serve one master? Were they actually working toward a common goal... a goal so secret that most members of these secret societies would live and die ignorant of the higher purpose they served?

A drop of blood splashed on the page directly on the line drawing of the altar. I shivered and nervously dabbed at my injured head with the handkerchief. I quickly turned page after page not daring to look up in case the librarian was still at hand and had witnessed my defiling the book. As I delved further into this tome of knowledge of good and evil, I caught a name that brought me up short: *Solomon*.

Gaston Max believed the Mad Arab, Prince Abard, had adopted the identity of the long-dead author of this very book. Prince Abard had claimed all I endured was for the Seal of Solomon. Thomas Valley had stated Freemasonry was founded by the builders of King Solomon's temple...

I could not turn to my father for advice and Sir Lionel Barton, the foremost Egyptologist of our day, was currently in North Africa off on another one of his infernal digs with no way of anyone reaching him. Of course, even if he had been at home in Greywater Park, his Norfolk manor with its menagerie of exotic beasts and even more exotic native servants, it would have done me little good in Paris. Yet, here in this great library, in this very book published by the very same publishing house that planned to reveal Reverend Eltham's secrets to an unsuspecting world, here was the answer to my remaining questions. I quickly scanned the next several pages for information.

*Solomon's Seal is the name given to the six-pointed star-like figure engraved on the bottom of Arab drinking cups.*

As I looked at the drawing of the figure, I recognized the Eastern icon Eltham had given me. The same icon I had attacked Kau with to win my freedom. Was this the Seal of Solomon? I read on.

*In 1001 Arabian Nights, Sinbad the Sailor presents Haroun al-Rashid with one such drinking cup depicting the Table of Solomon.*

There was a simple line drawing of what appeared to be the same drinking cup, but this one was engraved with the Table of Solomon. The Table was the same as that which appeared in the line drawing I had seen illustrated earlier in the book and among Kane Keller's hidden drawings. I could feel the perspiration running down my face as I continued reading.

*The Seal of Solomon is an ancient Jewish legend adopted and adapted over the centuries by the Arabs. It is very likely that the true source of the legend rests in Greek mythology. The earliest historical record of the Seal of Solomon is found in the First Century A.D. when Josephus notes Eleazar used a magic ring, formerly belonging to King Solomon, to exorcise demons in the presence of Vespasian.*

*The Seal of Solomon is the signet ring on which is engraved the Most Holy Name of God. It is a gift from the God of Abraham and is made of brass and iron. The magical properties of this ring allow the bearer to control demons or* jinns, *in Arab vernacular. King Solomon signed his written commands to the good* jinn *with the brass part of the ring and the evil jinn with the iron part in one of the earliest surviving examples of the alchemical elements in oral tradition.*

*The Arabs believed King Solomon received four such jewels from four different angels that visited him. Legends say Solomon set the jewels into one ring to control the Four Elements. The demon Asmodeus obtained possession of King Solomon's magic ring and cast it into the sea to deprive him of the power of exorcism. The ring was later discovered by an Arab fisherman and was passed down through the generations ever since. Fabricius believed this legend to be an adaptation of* Polycrates' Ring, *popularized by Herodotus.*

*The modern scholar, familiar with his Goethe, should recall the Drudenfuss from* Faust. *Drudenfuss (literally, 'the Druid's Foot' or Pentagram) prevented Mephistopheles from entering the house whose threshold it guarded. Bishop Kennet re-christened the Druid's Foot, the Pentangle of Solomon because its representation had the power to drive off demons.*

*The Seal of Solomon is the hieroglyphic representation of a devout follower raising his hands in adoration of God. Such images are mainly found in stone sepulchral steles. A number of representations of this image may be seen on display in the Louvre.*

I now realized this was the frontispiece of the book. The painting of the pale, featureless ghoul dressed in a bright purple tunic dancing was actually a devout follower of Yahweh raising his hands in adoration of God. I continued reading.

*This is the Form of the Secret Seal of Solomon, wherewith King Solomon did bind and seal up the aforesaid sprits and their legions in a vessel of brass. This Seal is to be made by one who is clean both inward and outward and hath not defiled himself by any woman in the space of a month, but hath in prayer and fasting desired of God to forgive him all of his sins. It is to be made on the day of Mars or Saturn at the stroke of midnight when the moon is in the Sign of Virgo. The Seal is to be written upon virgin parchment with the blood of a black cock that has never defiled a hen. When the Seal is so made, the bearer shall perfume the Seal with alum, sun-dried raisins, dates, cedar, and lignum aloes. By this Seal, the bearer thereby gains the love of all manner of men and is assured he will not fall to weapon, fire, or water.*

Instantly, I recalled what Eltham had long ago told me of the invincibility formula favored by the Boxers in China at the turn of the century. When a Boxer fell in battle, it was said that he had been an unbeliever and, therefore, unworthy of the protection of the gods. Likewise, the bearer of the Seal of Solomon who was felled in battle would be said to be unclean, having failed to adhere to the specific astrological requirements. Here again was the call to avoid that which was unclean. The puzzle was complete at last, but I still had no clue as to what the completed picture represented.

If the Seal of Solomon was real, who had it and why had Reverend Eltham died because of it? I might better understand this question if I had an actual copy of Eltham's manuscript. Thomas Valley believed that Neville McBride still had this manuscript and suggested Greba might have brought a copy with her from London. My God, what fate had I left Greba to? I had done my fair share of research, now was the time to act. I could not hide in a library forever. I must go out and face my destiny.

I closed the book shut and replaced it in its snug space on the lowest shelf and turned toward the stairs. Upon reaching the bottom of the grand marble staircase, my courage was deflated by the sight that greeted me. Gaston Max stood at the bottom of the stairwell flanked by a pair of grim-faced gendarmes. I was had.

## 21. ME AND GASTON MAX

"Where are we going?" I asked.

Gaston Max did not even glance at me as he replied, "The eternal question. *Quo Vadis*." There was no humor in his voice as he spoke. He continued to stare ahead of us as we raced along the Bois de Boulogne in a police cab.

Neither Max nor either of the gendarmes had spoken a word to me since I was hustled unceremoniously from the steps of the Bibliothèque Nationale to the astonished gasps and outraged pronouncements of dozens of respectable Parisians and taken away as if I were the infamous Fantômas, unmasked at last.

"You are going to the station," Gaston Max declared. "If you do precisely as you are told, you shall avoid imprisonment."

"You will find me an eager and enthusiastic student when it comes to avoiding Devil's Island. Please instruct me on how best to proceed."

My sarcasm won me a contemptible glance from the Frenchman.

"You are being taken to the train station. You will be given safe passage back to London. In a short while, the world shall learn that Greba Eltham, alone and distraught over the death of her father, has committed suicide in Paris. A note will be found that she had burned the only copy of her father's memoirs prior to ending her own life. Thomas Valley will subsequently announce that it will now prove impossible to publish her late father's book and the matter will be forgotten... as it should be."

I was aghast at his words.

"You... you mean to kill Greba?" I asked incredulously.

He glanced at me as if I were but a child and turned to stare ahead of me once more.

"Dr. Petrie, you should have learned by now that everyone in this world chooses their own fate. Those who dwell in darkness grow accustomed to the absence of light. There are no accidents. Each of us earns Heaven or Hell in our own time."

"You speak in riddles."

Gaston Max sighed, irritably. "I have told you before, man is constant, never changing. He seeks to defy God... to defeat Him, but it can never be. He seeks to replace Him with old ideas he thinks of new. They will never take. The Truth cannot be erased no matter how many may try. We can but delude ourselves for a time. Convince ourselves we have won when we were lost before we were conceived."

"You're a madman."

"Am I?" he asked. "You will learn otherwise if you live long enough. You judge me harshly because I am a Roman Catholic and you are an agnostic, yes? Do you not recall the parable of the scorpion and the frog?"

"I've never been much for children's stories... the Bible or otherwise."

"Your loss, *mon ami*. There is much wisdom to be had from parables." He smiled at me with a look that might have been one of affection. "There was once a frog that lived in the swamp. It came upon a scorpion that asked for safe passage to the outer bank. The frog declined this request reasoning that the scorpion would sting it and they would both perish. The scorpion shook its head and countered that such logic was unreasonable for if the scorpion stung the frog whilst crossing the swamp, the scorpion would drown. The frog considered his argument for a moment and decided that all that lives fights to preserve life. So the frog agreed to give the scorpion safe passage to the outer bank. Half way across the swamp, the scorpion stung the frog. As they both sank into the blackness of the waters, the frog, with its dying breath, asked the scorpion why it had done such an unreasonable thing. The scorpion shrugged its shoulders as it sank beneath the brackish waves and said, 'It is my nature, I am a scorpion.'

"Whether frog or scorpion, *mon ami*, Gaston Max does not intend to drown. Like you, I chose to wear the mantle of the Brotherhood of Magi because it is a means to an end… because it opens doors that would otherwise be impossible to find. I do not betray my God in my heart of hearts… with my words, yes… with my actions, maybe… but never in my heart. Such is the way of all who seek to dispel the forces of darkness. Each day… each hour spent in their presence stains one's soul a little bit more. One cannot fight in the mud without themselves becoming sullied. The grown up world functions by the same laws as the child's; we fool ourselves if we think it is otherwise."

"You have an eloquent tongue, Monsieur Max," I said. "However, I am afraid Dr. Fu Manchu has beaten you. Greba's blood will not be on your hands because it already stains his."

Gaston Max sighed a second time. "I have said you will learn that Greba Eltham has committed suicide. I have not said that she will actually do so. We retrieved Miss Eltham from the cab along with an injured servant of Fu Manchu's who was unconscious behind the wheel of the car."

"You mean to say that Greba is still alive?"

The Frenchman nodded. "I saw them both safely off to the Sûreté just before we converged on the Bibliothèque Nationale. The Chinaman was badly wounded. You can be quite savage when you are cornered. Little wonder that Dr. Fu Manchu respects you some small measure. I give you my word that Greba shall be given the same chance at freedom as I am giving you now. It is necessary that the world believe she has followed her father to the grave, for her sake. It is the only way. Were I to do otherwise, she would not even have the slightest hope of surviving."

"How do you intend to bring this business of Eltham's memoirs to a close?"

Gaston Max paused for a moment and did not look at me as he replied, "What I say to you now must be held in the strictest confidence. If you betray this trust, it will cost not only both our lives, but the life of Greba Eltham as well."

He reached to his feet and lifted a satchel. "Inside this bag is a parcel that was sent to me by Miss Eltham for safekeeping prior to her arrival in Paris. She intended to claim it once she was here, but you already know why that proved to be impossible for her to do."

He stared at me meaningfully until the truth dawned upon me at last.

"You have had the manuscript that Thomas Valley was searching for all along!"

He smiled slightly and nodded his head almost imperceptibly.

"Yes, I possess the manuscript and a second item of even greater value. Neither must be allowed to fall into the hands of Monsieur Valley, the Brotherhood of Magi, or the Si-Fan. It was these same items Prince Abard was willing to kill and die for. It was these same items that spelt doom for your friend, Reverend Eltham. It was these same items that sealed Greba's fate. That is why the world must believe her to be dead. There would be no peace for her were anyone to learn that these treasures yet exist."

"You must not destroy them! That manuscript holds the key to stopping Dr. Fu Manchu and ending his reign of terror!"

Gaston Max smiled. "That is why I am giving them to you to take back to London with you. There, you will see that Mr. Smith and Inspector Weymouth learn everything, even if they have never uttered the word *Bismillah* in their lives."

When we arrived at the station, I felt an almost palpable sense of hope for the first time in weeks. After I boarded the train and found my seat, I opened the satchel Gaston Max had entrusted to my care and withdrew the unpublished memoirs of J. D. Eltham. As I started to read, I found myself wondering whether I had chosen to play the part of the frog or the scorpion in this particular parable.

## 22. MAN O' GOD

*I shared the name of John Daniel Eltham with my father as he had with his father before him... My grandfather died when my father was barely nine... His boyhood was marred by mistreatment and despair, but he grew into a good man... My mother was a woman of great faith. A blacksmith's wife would never know luxury, but she found pleasure among her garden, her books, and my sister and me. She died just days before my 11th birthday. I was lost without her.*

*My sister was only 12 years old and soon found herself over-burdened with the demands of managing a household... It was only natural that I turned to the ministry as a young man... I was sincere in my vocation, but troubled by the emptiness I felt inside. I wanted to drown in my faith... So it was that I plunged in feet first as a missionary.*

*Meeting Freda changed me as much as her honesty and purity sustained me. I had not known love nor had I experienced its gnawing yearning until I set eyes upon her perfect face. She was beautiful, not in the sense that people misuse the word today, but in the true, classical definition of the quality. Her hair was spun with gold and bronzed burning embers. Her eyes were soft and trusting. Her smile was guileless and could warm the coldest heart as it warmed mine. I loved her the moment I glimpsed her. I love her now and wish she were still by my side.*

*That was how it ended. The beginning was one of hope.*

*It was our daughter Greba's eighth birthday when we learned my next assignment was to be Nan-Yang in China... Freda looked as beautiful as the day she became my bride as she stood clinging to the ship's rail whilst Greba waved goodbye to the party gathered on the dock as our little family prepared to begin a new life together in a strange land.*

*I was not the first Christian missionary to come to China. There had been many attempts to bring the Word of Christ to its people for the past two centuries. The Empire had left its mark even in this remote part of the world in the form of the paved roads, hospitals, schools, orphanages, and churches that offered us our only sense of comfort as we made our way to Nan-Yang.*

*The rocky terrain and mud-covered trails that separate the rice fields made our travel even more onerous once the paved roads became less frequent. More than once Freda and I sank waist-deep in the muddy path and were forced to hold little Greba above our heads until we worked our way free. Fallen trees frequently forced detours into the dense, impenetrable forests... The constant rainfall floods the rivers. It was impossible for us to cross a river by horse for fear the animals would be carried downstream by the current and drowned... This was where our little family put down roots in February 1896... I would be lying if I said I didn't wish we were back home much of the time... Even dreary old England does not know the tedium of the ceaseless rains that plague China.*

*We soon learned much of China is comprised of isolated villages with their own unique customs, style of dress, and language... Nan-Yang means "South Sun" and rests between the south side of Mount Dushan and the north side of the Baihe River... The people of Nan-Yang sleep in make-shift shacks that shelter them from the punishing sun... These shacks are little more than thatched roofs supported by bamboo poles with blankets thrown over the sides to serve as walls... Pine boxes are the only furniture to be found on the dirt floors.*

*Men and women in the village live apart... The women eat scraps when there are any... Their homes are unequally divided into quarters with each provided their own separate entrance. Any man who enters a woman's quarter is severely punished... As they have no traditions regarding celibacy, it is surprising that more of the villagers aren't polygamous.*

*Months passed without a convert among the villagers. The people of Nan-Yang were too busy planting rice to have time for God. My Sunday services were barely attended because the people were too busy working; even the women and children... Those who shirk their chores are severely punished.*

*All Chinese people smoke, even the children, for Chinese people lack any concept of moderation. They smoke whenever they can afford it and as often as they are able... The villagers showered Freda, Greba, and me with gifts of tobacco.*

*Had I only preached, I would have been wasting my time. I found my purpose caring for the sick and the aged in the makeshift hospital I constructed in the village with Freda and sometimes even Greba acting as my nurse. Many of the villagers were starving, anemic, and plagued with scabies, body odor, and fetid breath. Their poor condition was reflected in their small stature and swollen and bloodied feet.*

*Malaria is very common in rural China. Hospitals are too scattered for these people and there is little medicine and even less quinine to be found. Before our arrival, the sick of Nan-Yang sought witch doctors who told them to sacrifice cattle to be cured of their ills. When that failed to work, the people turned to opium for relief... Opium allows them to sleep despite their fever. Some die addicted to the drug while others survive the fever only to carry their new vice to the grave.*

*The Chinese have a wise saying: "Man with opium habit cannot work." Men with the opium habit will sometimes sell their wife and children to obtain the drug. Many of the women in Nan-Yang end up homeless, unable to care for themselves and their children, when their addicted husbands abandon them to their fate. These women would prefer to see their children raised as Christians than see them share their father's fate, but the women themselves have no desire to convert.*

*When we visit a sick villager's home, it is customary for the host to offer his visitors a foot massage. Freda would always gratefully accept their hospitality as her feet never recovered from the many days we were forced to travel on foot when we first arrived... The villagers study my features with uncommon interest and ask ridiculous questions such as whether I know how much water the Baihe River holds. Hesitation to respond is tantamount to inviting their mockery.*

*I spent many nights sitting cross-legged by the campfire enjoying my pipe while lost in thought. Even by the warmth of the campfire it is necessary for Freda and me to drape a blanket about our shoulders to protect ourselves against the disease-carrying mosquitoes which would otherwise bite through the fabric of our shirts. The comfortable life we left behind in England was but a memory, Nan-Yang was the real world now.*

*Sleep did not come easily most nights. The incessant snoring of the villagers and the sound of their horses' tails swatting gnats from outside disturbed Freda and Greba. The spirits of evil were as real as the immensity of the dangerous forest that surrounds Nan-Yang. The rustling of the leaves would set my nerves on edge for fear some unseen predator would come for us in the night.*

*Many mornings, I would be jolted awake hours before sunrise by the sound of torch-bearing villagers laughing and singing merrily on their way to fish in the Baihe River. As a child, Greba would easily sleep through such common disturbances and her poor mother was usually so exhausted, nearly nothing could disturb her hard-won early morning slumber. I would quietly clamber outside and stir the fire that I had left burning through the night to ward off any wild beasts of the forest.*

*The bonze from the nearest pagoda would sometimes come to visit. He felt kinship to me, yet he always avoided discussing my religion. He had been the bonze for nearly 15 years when Freda and I first met him and had long since grown tired of teaching the people about the Maitreya Buddha who waited in the Tusita to bring paradise to Earth. He told me many neighboring villages no longer had a pagoda because the people had ceased to care about tradition.*

*On one of his visits, his conversation turned to the White Lotus secret society which he blamed for drawing many of the faithful away from the old traditions. The White Lotus Society was devoted to Wu Sheng Lao Mu, the Eternal Venerable Mother whom they believed wept over her followers in her longing to bring them to their eternal home. The White Lotus group practiced faith healing in the Unborn Old Mother's name, meditated on her life daily, and chanted the mantra of True Emptiness in her honor.*

*The followers of Buddha Amitabha, the Buddha of Light were equally numerous in the regions surrounding Nan-Yang. The bonze also mentioned a secret society that I had never heard of at the time called I Ho Ch'uan, the Righteous Harmonious Fists. I thought little of any of these groups then apart from reflecting that had my mission been successful, I too would have constituted a threat to the old traditions the bonze represented.*

*Some weeks later, the bonze returned. He appeared fragile and worn. He warned me to take Freda and Greba and return home. He said it would not be safe soon for any Westerners to remain in China. I laughed off his concerns, secure that the people of Nan-Yang had accepted us for the good deeds we did for them.*

*He spoke of I Ho Ch'uan once more. He told me how they had driven the Jesuits out of China 150 years before and were preparing to drive the Christians out again. Once more, I was unmoved for there are always those opposed to the changes missionaries bring who resort to force and intimidation in their effort to preserve tradition.*

*What I did not then know was that Prince Tuan of the Imperial Court of the Dowager Empress was counted among this group's numbers and the Empress herself* was a silent supporter of their cause. China's recent defeat in their foolhardy war with Japan and two successive failed crops was enough to convince the people they had fallen from the favor of their gods. The widespread famine and the plague of locusts that followed naturally in the wake of the failed crops only confirmed this belief. The Yellow River flooded hundred of villages. The sheer number of German, Russian, French, and English missionaries in China was leading to a growing resentment of all foreigners.

None of this was yet known to me. There was only the bonze and his fears that the Boxers, as I Ho Ch'uan were more commonly known, had become nearly invulnerable and were growing in popular support across the country each day. I thought the invulnerability he spoke of referred only to their swelling ranks, but the bonze insisted that the Boxers could survive bullets fired into their chests at close range thanks to the incantation of their shamans who placed them in protective trances before battle.

I laughed at the very thought of such superstitious nonsense, but the bonze became even more grave and with shaking hands produced a small leather pouch from beneath his robes. Within the pouch there was a ring. Trembling hands held it out to me as if he feared exposing it to the light. I turned the ring over in my hands. It was doubtless of great antiquity and certainly not of Chinese origin given the nature of the ideographs that decorated it, but otherwise harmless. I tried returning it to the bonze, but he insisted I keep it and laughing nervously, made a hurried departure for his pagoda.

Here was the crux of my problem. The bonze was unquestionably the most educated man in Nan-Yang and yet he behaved like a frightened child when confronted with the unknown, no matter how innocuous the object. I gave the ring to Greba who was delighted with her little treasure and took to wearing it day and night.

My heart was saddened by her small pleasure for it only emphasized the miserable childhood my station had afforded her that such a worthless piece of metal might rank as a keepsake valued above all others in this God-forsaken country. Freda wisely cautioned Greba to have a care to keep her treasured ring out of sight for if the bonze responded so strongly to the sight of a foreign ring, there would be no telling what the reaction of the simple villagers of Nan-Yang might be.

The bonze's words proved prophetic for soon I began to hear disturbing talk among the villagers of scandalous tales of the terrible abuse of Chinese women and children perpetrated by Western missionaries. The foulest, most disgusting images were conjured, but the villagers were quick to assure me they had no doubt that I was not one of these white devils posing as men of peace.

My friend, the bonze, was likewise a man of peace. When his pagoda was burned a few days later and his severed head found displayed on a pike outside the village, the talk among the people of Nan-Yang turned quickly from outrage and fear to speculation he had stolen something of great value from I Ho Ch'uan to an acceptance his death served as an example of the fate awaiting those who befriend Christians. He had been right to tell me to flee the country while I had the chance. Now it was too late.

China was aflame. There would be no safe passage for Freda, Greba, and me while the Boxers began their purge. Many homes and businesses were burned to the ground. The Dowager Empress issued an imperial edict *defending the Boxers against all charges of criminal wrongdoing. There were organized riots in the face of threats of military reprisals from Western diplomats. The telegraph line from Peking to Pao Ting Fu was cut. The Feng Tai railway junction was burned. Imperial troops were openly collaborating with the Boxers. Peking was under siege.*

*I knew none of this until much later. What I knew the morning I awoke to a group of torch-bearing men coming down the path before sunrise was they were not gathering to go fishing in the Baihe River. They were instead gathered outside our home shouting "sha, sha" ("kill, kill"). It was the morning of June 16, 1899 and I would have thanked God in Heaven for an attack by the wild beasts of the forest that I lived in fear of for it would have been a less frightening prospect than herding my startled wife and daughter out the back door of our burning home to seek refuge in our little bamboo hospital where we had restored life to countless villagers and their children lo these past several years.*

*We stayed there for what seemed an eternity. The rations were minimal. None came to offer us aid. We lived in fear of showing ourselves or making a sound. I do not know whether it was a matter of weeks or days. We lived like starving rats while the Siege of Peking raged many miles away and the combined military forces of Europe, Great Britain, and the United States fought their way to end this madness. We knew nothing of this shred of hope and, truth be told, there was little relief it could have brought us in Nan-Yang had the news travelled so far from the Forbidden City.*

*It is a matter of history that the Manchu Dynasty teetered on the brink of collapse in December 1900. Prince Tuan would face exile. I Ho Ch'uan would be disbanded and anti-foreignism would be made a crime punishable by death. The Boxer Rebellion would officially end with the signing of the peace treaty on September 7, 1901, but this was not even a faint hope while I hid in darkness believing the Creator of the Universe, if He existed, was cruel and capricious and deserving only of fear and contempt for abandoning a missionary and his wife and daughter in a land of madness and death.*

*The Boxers came to Nan-Yang as I knew they would. The three of us had crawled on our bellies like insects. Our skin was covered in the grime of dirt, mud, and our own urine and excrement. Our clothes were naught but filthy rags. We had done nothing to incite them, yet the Boxers came just the same and the good people of Nan-Yang stood as one with them shouting, "sha, sha" and demanding we show ourselves and be killed.*

*I told Freda to take Greba and prepare to run. I would offer a distraction and lead the Boxers away as best I could. We would meet up again at the burned remains of the bonze's pagoda on the outskirts of the village. Greba panicked and ran off, insisting in a frightened child's foolish madness that she could not leave without her treasured ring. Freda ran after her, shouting her name hysterically. I could hear the sounds of the barricaded hospital door splitting beneath the weight of the angry mob. The wood splintered and the door gave way, the Boxers poured through and came to a sudden halt when they saw I was not running.*

*I had not stood as a man for so long. I was facing death, yet I felt no fear. I did not have the Lord's protection to strengthen me. I did not want His aid, what I had to do this day would be done with my bare hands or not at all.*

*I looked at my enemies and smiled. I felt the warmth of anger coursing through my veins. I spoke in tongues. My speech was a garbled mixture of English, German, and Cantonese for my brain was on fire and I knew soon I would lose the ability to think and reason as a man. Primal instinct was taking over and I welcomed it.*

*"You vile despicable filth," I cried. "You dare to corner me like an animal. I treated you with compassion and humanity. I taught you, healed you, nurtured you, and now you hunt me down to kill me. You diseased, drug-addled, degenerate yellow pricks. I treated you as if you had dignity and worth. I lived the lie that you were my equals. You superstitious, simple-minded, simpering scum. You could not fathom that I was the spirit who stole into your homes at night and smashed your precious Buddha to the ground. It was I who desecrated your shrines to your pathetic pagan deities. You would not listen to the Truth of Christ's message if your lives depended on it. Even after I burned your pagoda to the ground and killed that useless fool of a bonze for daring to confront me, still you wouldn't hear the Truth. You are animals. Yellow, hairless apes with your inarticulate speech and your hideous little faces. My God, I've hated you from the moment I arrived and so help me, God; I'll hate each and every one of you as I kill you today with my bare hands."*

*I burned evermore with an inner fire that could be contained, but never extinguished. Somehow, they understood enough of my words to react. They overcame their fear and with a single hideous scream, they charged me. There is a Yellow Fever in the Orient. Some men die of it and it took hold of me at that moment to my everlasting shame. I did not stay and face my enemies stoically; I turned tail and ran like a frightened blubbering child. I ran for my life.*

The train screeched to a halt at the station. Exhausted, I put the manuscript away. The hours had passed quickly as I delved deeper into Eltham's strange and terrible madness. I had not even chanced upon the passage where he learned of Freda's cruel fate at the hands of the Boxers or of his life-changing introduction to theosophy. I was grateful for the interruption. His memoirs were consumed with blackness and despair. If the disease that claimed his soul was spread throughout the world, there would be no limit to the evil that man could do.

I had learned more from Eltham's past than he himself could have ever hoped to learn. I knew that the other priceless item inside the battered leather pouch Greba had posted to Gaston Max for safekeeping was the very same signet ring that had been given to Eltham by that poor old bonze. I knew the strange ideographs carved upon it without ever having seen them. I knew that the ring Greba prized in her childhood was not the useless trinket that her father believed it to be.

I also knew that Eltham's memoirs revealed something far more sinister than Dr. Fu Manchu's true identity. For Eltham unwittingly had stumbled upon the secret of the Boxer Uprising. He had unwittingly stumbled upon the secret of the Si-Fan. He had discovered the same secret that now brought the Brotherhood of Magi and the Si-Fan together. Reverend Eltham had given Greba nothing less than the mystical Seal of Solomon itself as a keepsake and the whole world might perish for his folly.

## 23. DUCK TO EAT

As I departed the Folkestone Express and stepped onto the station platform, I felt a great weight suddenly give way and I instantly knew the relief of being home again. London at Christmas never really changes. It is the same now as it was when I was a boy. The city has always been the only place in the world where I felt a keen sense of identity.

I shivered with excitement as I stepped into one of the waiting cabs at the station and asked the driver to deposit me at The Fox and Anchor. The pub had long served as our rendezvous in London and I was eager to bring Nayland Smith up to date on all that had occurred during my sojourn in Paris. As usual, I felt a pang of disappointment as I stepped out of the cab and found him to be nowhere in sight. It was always my custom to wait outside for his arrival whilst he preferred to get a table and wait for me indoors.

The Christmas season and the inclement weather meant the place was unusually crowded. Smith had still managed to find a table in one of our usual spots next to the large front window. Typical of him, he had claimed the chair facing the window and left me with my back to that enchanting view of Yuletide London.

"Smith!" I cried, stretching out my hand to grasp his warmly.

"Hello, old man," he said, solemnly. "Have a seat, have a seat. You're a welcome sight as always… these days, even more so."

"Have you ordered yet, Nayland?" I said sitting down and opening my menu.

"Hmm?" he asked absentmindedly, mouth clenched fast to the end of his unlit pipe.

Half-starved and more than a bit homesick, I had quickly lost myself in the menu and was barely aware as I mumbled my response to him.

"Don't think I want smoked salmon today. Rather tired of it. Anything you care to suggest, Smith?"

"Duck!" he yelled as he flipped the table over into my lap whilst diving towards me with both arms outstretched as if he were plunging off a pier for a brisk morning swim.

Everything happened so quickly that it is difficult to recall the precise sequence of events. Somehow, I was jarred by the sound of shattering glass and the frightened cries of dismay by our fellow patrons. Nayland Smith grasped me by my lapels with a single hand and dragged me along behind him like a child. He rolled our table sideways like a giant wheel with his free hand in an effort to provide some shelter from the stampeding patrons who thoughtlessly knocked into one another as the pub descended into absolute chaos.

Gradually it dawned upon me that Smith looked as frightened as everyone around us. I stole a quick glance back to where we had been seated to see if the source of this nightmarish cacophony could be found. My blood froze in my veins when I saw them.

Six snowmen stood in the restaurant, surveying the havoc their violent arrival had created. Shards of broken glass clung to thick, matted ivory fur where the front window had shattered under the force of their violent entry. Fur! The word stuck in my throat like a walnut. These weren't snowmen like the one that hid Eltham's lifeless form or those that contained the corpses of those unfortunate victims found on McBride's front lawn. These were living creatures neither man nor bear, but rather something in between.

Their faces were featureless. Only a slight indentation in that blank mound of snow white fur betrayed the existence of eyes and a mouth. The six monstrosities lumbered through the restaurant overturning tables, smashing wine bottles, and sending plates of food flinging against walls and scattering across the floor. They did not utter a sound or give off an odor, but otherwise they were as savage as the beasts one can find caged in the zoo.

*This is madness*, I thought. *What was that accursed word... Bismil? No, that wasn't it. Bismis? God, why couldn't I recall it?*

I just had time to register a heavy wooden table hurtling toward me through the air like some great javelin when Smith ploughed into the back of my legs and felled me seconds before the impact would surely have knocked me senseless.

"When I tell you to duck, I mean duck!" he hissed in my ear.

I stood staring at his face for a moment. I realized he was listening intently... to what? There was nothing but silence now. Slowly, Smith raised himself up off the ground and then signaled for me to do likewise.

The creatures were gone. Cold winter air blew through the broken front window. The restaurant was a shambles, but the snowmen had disappeared. Smith ran forward and carefully clambered through the broken glass and shattered wooden frame that had once afforded the Fox and Anchor a perfect view of the busy London traffic.

"Smith, wait!" I cried, but he had already vanished out of view.

Cautiously, I followed his trail. I had not anticipated being outside without my overcoat and hat. The icy wind pawed at my exposed flesh like the remorseless beggars that crowd the marketplaces in Egypt. I rounded the corner just as the headlamps from a parked lorry unexpectedly came to life, temporarily blinding me. The engine roared and the lorry accelerated rapidly, forcing me to hug the lamppost as the lorry tore past.

Smith hurried back to where I stood, frozen and trembling, at the mouth of the alleyway.

"Did you see the driver of that lorry, Petrie?"

I shook my head no as I tried to stop my shivering tongue from cursing.

"They were Oriental." He breathed heavily into cupped hands as his teeth audibly chattered. "I only caught a glimpse of them, but I'm bloody well sure of it. Our snowmen are Orientals."

"Orientals? How is that possible?"

Smith grimaced in irritation, "Think, man. Those weren't animals that descended upon us back there. Those were men. No paw prints, no smell, no snarls. I've been waiting for this to happen. I suspected as much and now that I've seen them, I'm sure of it."

"Sure of what? What are you on about, Smith? How could you have known to expect something as bizarre as this to happen?"

Nayland looked at me in amazement, before his furrowed brow softened and his steely blue-grey eyes disappeared in the creases of his smile.

"Of course, how could I have forgotten? You've been in Paris. You couldn't have known."

Without warning, Smith darted across the street to where a newsboy stood on the opposite corner. I watched as he paid the boy and ran back with a folded newspaper clenched beneath one arm.

"Here!"

Smith pressed the newspaper to my chest. The wind blew each corner of the paper in every direction. I did my best to cling to it as we walked back to the Fox and Anchor and pushed our way through the crowd gathered outside the entrance.

Waiters were busy sweeping up broken glass and collecting fragments of splintered wood. Strange as it may sound now, we ignored the madness that surrounded us and sought refuge at a small table near the kitchen that had been left intact. As we sat down, Smith took the newspaper from me and spread it down upon the table. He paged through it rapidly with growing impatience.

"Here! Have a look." He said, tapping furiously at the paper as he turned it to face my direction.

*SIX SNOWMEN SIGHTED IN SUSSEX*, the article proclaimed boldly.

"Nearly every day there's been another one like it."

Smith turned the paper back his way before I could read more of the article.

"Some of the sightings are doubtless just the baseless ramblings of simpleminded attention-seekers, but there have been several incidents like what occurred here tonight. No one has ever been harmed, just property damage. Always the same story... The six snowmen vanish into thin air as if they were night phantasms. Someone is using these snowmen to hold London in a grip of fear and thus far, they are succeeding. There is a purpose behind these acts of terror and we're going to get to the root of it."

"I think I already know what is at the root of it, Smith," I said.

"What? Good Lord, Petrie!" he cried, slapping a hand to his forehead. "Don't hesitate another second, man. Tell me what you learned in Paris."

I related it all to Smith, as he sat listening with rapt attention, every detail from my meeting with poor Greba Eltham to the terrible fate of Keenan Pethig and what we found hidden in Kane Keller's apartment. I recounted the horrible night Greba tried to kill me and my introduction to the remarkable Gaston Max. I described, in great detail, our first encounter with Thomas Valley and the awful punishment Aziz inflicted on him at the *Lapin Agile*. I relived my abduction by *Les Apaches* and all that had followed with Prince Abard, Fu Manchu, Kara, those poor children, and that hideous crocodile. I told Smith of the secret bond that held me and Gaston Max to Thomas Valley; of my dream of a visitation by Daniel Eltham's ghost, the all too real icon that Eltham had given me, and the secret word that just as suddenly had disappeared from my mind. Finally, I spoke of how I came to possess Eltham's manuscript and of the fabled Seal of Solomon that was the mysterious key to all of these terrible events.

"Well," I said resting back in my chair. "Not bad for a Paris holiday, eh?"

Smith's eyes twinkled and he fumbled for his pipe until he realized it had been lost in the chaos of the Snowmen's attack.

"Petrie, you are quite remarkable. Doctor, author, detective. I sometimes think you could do anything if you put your mind to it."

I felt my face redden at his praise.

"Now allow me to enlighten you where I am able," he continued. "You're not the only one who has been working on this case, you know. You'll recall the papers that you found folded in your jacket pocket the night that

Weymouth discovered you wandering around in a fog at Redmoat?"

I nodded my assent.

Smith reached into his pocket and withdrew the folded papers that he had spoken of and placed them in front of me on the table.

"The author of these papers states that he is only able to write in his native Chinese. He learned to speak English from a missionary many years ago. During the Boxer Uprising, he had his tongue torn from his mouth and his face carved as a punishment when he dared to defend the wife of a missionary friend as she was attacked and murdered before his very eyes. The Boxers tried to burn him alive for his noble actions. Miraculously, he escaped death, but not without paying a terrible price. Scarred and disfigured, he did not let these impairments hold him back. He became a doctor and proudly helps many of his fellow Chinamen and their families.

"He goes on to state that he has now undertaken to travel from China in an attempt to save the life of his old missionary friend whom he has not seen lo these many years. It seems that our Chinese friend is a member, probably only a low-ranking one, but a member in good standing nonetheless, of a powerful secret society. This same secret society has been searching for an object of great antiquity and power. They believe the very same missionary our Chinese friend is seeking possesses this object or has knowledge of where to find it. Our Chinese friend believes this missionary is likely ignorant of the object's true worth. I believe this fills in the remaining gaps in your own narrative."

My mind reeled at his words.

"Good God, Smith! The missionary is Eltham. The missionary's wife whose death the Chinaman witnessed was Freda Eltham. The object being sought by this secret society the Chinaman also belongs to is the Seal of Solomon."

Smith nodded his head.

"Yes, Petrie. The Chinaman who gave you these papers is the same man you glimpsed on the night you believed you encountered Eltham's ghost. This same Chinaman is the disfigured mute who nearly succeeded in rescuing you and Greba after tracking the both of you to Paris."

"Oh God, the Chinaman is Kau! I attacked him in that cab outside the hospital. Gaston Max arrested him for the attempted abduction of Greba Eltham. If he betrayed the Si-Fan to try to save us, he's a dead man. No prison cell will keep him safe from their vengeance! I couldn't have known... I couldn't have guessed that his intentions were pure. I need to contact Gaston Max. My head is reeling, Smith. What does it all mean? Did I really see Eltham's ghost? What of the secret password I was told? The same word that was used to hypnotize Greba and Thomas Valley. The same password used by the Brotherhood of Magi. I cannot tell reality from illusion. I'm lost, Smith. I'm utterly, hopelessly lost."

Smith moved his chair closer to the table making an awful groaning sound in its wake as the wooden legs scraped against the floor.

"Lower your voice, man. This is not a conversation for others' ears. The mere fact that you can no longer recall this secret password is significant. It means their hold on you has been broken somehow."

"Then you believe I was under hypnotic influence just as Greba and Valley were?"

"Of course," Smith snapped. "How else do you account for your having seen a dead man's ghost?"

"Then whoever really gave me that icon and told me the Arabic word also had access to Greba and Thomas Valley. Not only did they fall under its spell, but Valley believed it to be the password used by the... the..."

I faltered as the memory returned to me.

"What is it, Petrie? What do you recall?"

"Gaston Max told me to make sure under no circumstances that Eltham's manuscript or the Seal of Solomon ever be allowed to fall into the hands of the Brotherhood of Magi. It was Thomas Valley who invited us to Esteban Milagro's party at the *Lapin Agile*, but we found him with Prince Abard instead. Gaston Max suspected Esteban Milagro was disguising himself as an Arab prince and yet, that cannot be for I later learned Esteban Milagro's true identity in the Bibliothèque Nationale. He is the author of a book recently reprinted by McBride & Valley."

"So?"

"Smith, the book was first published 200 years ago!"

Smith smacked his hand down upon the table.

"Great Scott, Petrie! That's not all. You're forgetting we have only Thomas Valley's word that he and McBride are no longer in league with one another. That is certainly not the impression McBride gave us when we last spoke with him and Ursula Trelawney."

"No, that's true, but why should we trust a man of Neville McBride's character? Thomas Valley was certainly searching for Greba's copy of the manuscript for a reason. Granted, that doesn't explain why Gaston Max was so adamant that the Brotherhood of Magi not get a hold of it. Greba is no less a part of the puzzle for she told me that a man called Fulton Denison was responsible for her father's death and yet Gaston Max claims she told him that the man responsible for her father's death was called

Esteban Milagro. Max believed this Esteban Milagro to be an important figure in the Paris criminal underground, while Valley claimed that Fulton Denison was the man who introduced McBride to Eltham. What's more, the night I was hypnotized in Redmoat was the same night I first glimpsed Kau. We now know Kau to be a member of the Si-Fan, so can we truly trust him? It is absolutely infuriating trying to discern the truth in this tangled web of deception."

Smith leaned back in his chair and ran a hand through his hair in exasperation.

"A fair point, Petrie... actually, several fair points. Consider the fact that McBride was not able to supply the Home Office with anything other than an excerpt of Eltham's memoirs. I would suggest that there is only one copy of those memoirs in existence and Greba managed to get a hold of it before any of the others."

"Ursula Trelawney was living at Redmoat with Eltham at the time of his death; surely, she would have been the person most likely to discover the manuscript if that were the case, Smith."

"True, but she was also involved with Neville McBride as we saw the night we visited his home in Dartford. Who can say that she didn't flit back and forth between two lovers? I would hardly be surprised to learn that she did just that. Consequently, Ursula Trelawney may not have been in a position to get her hands on Eltham's manuscript either, particularly if he had just completed it as he told you the evening before he died. The other point worth noting is the confusion over the two names Greba gave in identifying the man she blamed for her father's death. By the time Greba met you on the way to Paris, she was likely already under hypnotic control.

Don't forget the man on the train... what was his name again?"

He snapped his fingers twice in irritation.

"Pethig. Keenan Pethig."

"Right. He and the cook are likely mixed up in this somewhere."

"Then why was he killed?"

"Petrie, you're not thinking clearly. Both of these groups... the Si-Fan and the Brotherhood of Magi... they are competing for the same object... the Seal of Solomon. One is not about to sit back and let the other gain the advantage if it can be helped."

"So what are you suggesting, Smith? Was Esteban Milagro the name of the man who led Eltham away from the ministry and into the Brotherhood of Magi? Was he the criminal that Gaston Max was seeking? Was he Prince Abard or is he someone we don't know who is still at large?"

Smith laughed and shook his head.

"I can't answer your questions yet, Petrie. The point is that by the time you met Greba, someone had determined an additional layer of deception was required to keep the charade afloat a little while longer. We are closer to unraveling the truth and we know that the signet ring that Greba has kept since childhood is somehow the key to it all. Although why I can't imagine, as its authenticity has never been established and the magical properties attributed to it are clearly nothing more than primitive folklore. Where is the icon Eltham's ghost supposedly gave you now?"

I panicked for a moment as I thought of what I should say.

"I... I must have dropped it when I attacked Kau in the cab that picked Greba and I up from the hospital."

"Yes, and deposited you at the steps of the Bibliothèque Nationale as you said. If Gaston Max has Kau and Greba, then it is reasonable to suppose that he has the ring. It was your finding the Milagro book in the Bibliothèque Nationale that we have to thank for ending the hypnotic influence over you."

"That may be, Smith," I said. "In fact, it is quite likely. I only wish I could believe that some of the more horrific moments of the past few weeks had been hypnotic illusions as well. I could have done without actually witnessing Keenan Pethig's awful death or discovering Eltham's corpse or learning of those five unknown men that were found encased in snow."

Smith frowned. "I'm glad that you brought up those five murdered men, Petrie. Their identities are no longer unknown to us."

"What?" I gasped.

"The identification came through whilst you were in Paris. Five missing persons cases: Stock, Nast, Cassell, Doran, and Jenkins. There's a common factor: they were all missionaries in China at the turn of the century."

"Good Heavens!" I exclaimed. "That places them in the same vicinity as Eltham during the same period of time. This could tie their deaths to the Seal of Solomon."

"Yes, Petrie, it does just that. Not only did all six men serve as missionaries in China at the time of the Boxer Uprising, but the other five were likely killed before Eltham as a process of elimination in trying to locate that blasted signet ring."

"If only we understood the significance of that unaccountable irritation to their foreheads. There's something else, Smith. If the Si-Fan hid six dead bodies in snowmen, why would they subsequently send six of their men round to wreck havoc all over London disguised as living snowmen?"

Smith shrugged. "Why choose snowmen at all? The strange deaths laid at the feet of the Si-Fan only point to two reasons if past experience is anything to judge by... obscuring the truth and spreading terror. The spectacle of six Orientals dressed as snowmen destroying McBride's home or the Fox and Anchor or St. Bart's in the wee hours of the morning satisfies the second criteria certainly, but not enough to appease my skepticism. I think otherwise, Petrie, but I don't have enough information to be sure."

"I hadn't considered that it might have been the six snowmen who ransacked McBride's home just hours after we left it."

Smith tugged at his earlobe. "It certainly resembles their work here and it makes sense once you consider the fact that the Si-Fan had a motive in obscuring the Brotherhood of Magi's involvement with those Chinese prostitutes that we glimpsed through the window during that orgy at McBride's residence. The Ghost Brides, I believe that Chinaman told you they were called. Another point, Petrie, is the one clue that we have not investigated in Eltham's murder."

"What clue, Smith? What could you and Weymouth have possibly of overlooked?"

Smith rapped the table with his forefinger.

"The snake, Petrie. The snake and Ursula Trelawney's unexplained disappearance. Both point to a secret passage in Redmoat as does your disappearance from Limehouse before you turned up in what was likely some unknown part of Redmoat where you were subjected to hypnotic influence in the first place."

"I understand where you're heading with this, Smith, but I don't see how we could have missed finding a hidden room. We both looked for one and found nothing... nor did Weymouth."

"That only proves it is well-hidden, not non-existent, Petrie. There is a severe limitation to the rational science you subscribe to, I hope you realize that fact one day before it is the death of you."

"Fine, Smith. There is a secret passage as yet undetected. What advantage do we have today that we lacked at the time?"

"McBride is our advantage," Smith beamed.

I shook my head in frustration as I waited for him to elaborate on the point.

"You recall that foul handkerchief he blew his nose in repeatedly, don't you? What does that suggest to your mind?"

"A winter cold and poor personal hygiene," I replied.

Smith laughed. "Poor old Petrie. Once you've had your pride bruised, you shut down your mental faculties entirely. You're more your father's son than you allow yourself to imagine. Don't think twice about it now. If I'm right, you'll see the light soon enough. Fancy a visit to Redmoat tonight, Petrie? It is Christmas Eve, after all. Who knows? We may even get our fortunes told."

## 24. THE GARDEN OF DELIGHTS

The frozen ground crunched beneath our feet as Smith and I pushed our way through the frost-covered shrubbery. The intricate labyrinth of bushes and elms hid Redmoat from view to all but those most familiar with the forest-shrouded banks of the Waverney. As always, we looked for the familiar signposts of irregularly shaped elms or shrubs to help keep our bearings.

"Wait here, Petrie," Smith hissed.

He broke off in a trot as the shrubbery parted and revealed the moat that was Redmoat's namesake. The creepers and snaking tendrils that lie dead from the cold all along the perimeter served as an ever-present reminder that the moat had long since been drained and transformed into a garden. There was no one to tend to it now that Eltham and his staff were gone. There had been none to protect the plants from the savage onslaught of the autumnal cold and the newly arrived winter snow.

Smith grasped one of the creepers and began lowering himself into the moat. I stood anxiously watching for some sign of him. I felt a chill as I stood alone and vulnerable for what felt like half an hour, but was probably only a few minutes. Finally, I saw the creeper tighten and sway until Smith's head appeared above the side of the moat. He motioned with one hand for me to follow.

Cautiously, I began to follow him down. My footing slipped several times on the cold, damp, crumbling interior wall. I felt sure the creeper would break under the strain of our combined weight, but we successfully reached the floor of the moat in little more than a couple of minutes.

Smith was shining a torch beam along the bottom of the moat. He stopped occasionally to feel his way around the wall, poking and prodding at the loose masonry. So absorbed was he in his task that he seemed oblivious to the fact that I was following, albeit hesitantly, close behind him.

"What are you looking for, Smith?" I whispered as loudly as I dared.

He turned and glared at me as if I had asked a question so obvious, it insulted both our intelligence.

"A passageway, of course," he snapped.

"Why down here at the bottom of the moat?" I asked. "Wouldn't we be better served searching the house as we did before?"

Smith stopped and extinguished the torch.

"We're unlikely to find anything in there that we were unable to find before." He sighed in frustration. "That is why we came in through the moat."

"Again, I cannot fathom why you would expect to find a passage letting out into the bottom of the moat."

I knew I was risking Smith's temper, but I felt compelled to press on.

"I told you before, Petrie," Smith spoke through gritted teeth as he shone the torch on the wall in front of us. "McBride's filthy handkerchief was our clue."

I was about to protest once more when Smith's grip slipped on a crumbling piece of masonry in front of us and a short section of the wall below, no more than four feet from the ground, swung inwards and revealed an entry way apparently designed to allow access for a small child. Smith crouched down and shone the torch into the blackness of the passageway and then, dropping to all fours, he began crawling through the miniature doorway. Feeling more than a bit foolish, I imitated his stance and began to follow along behind him.

The passageway was tight and sloped uphill. Our movements were cramped and our progress was slow. I struggled to follow the glimmer of light that shone but a few feet ahead of me. While the torch beam remained static as I pressed onward, I was at least sure that the passageway did not taper leaving us trapped with naught but the thin air in the passage and the smell and touch of the cold dirt all around us.

Pebbles of soil were dropping into my hair as my head grazed the roof of the passageway. The dirt dug its way beneath my fingernails and stained my palms and the knees of my trousers as I crawled. I coughed several times and felt the dirt scratching my throat. There was a disconcerting sense of imbalance as it became evident we were crawling at an ever-widening angle and were now moving nearly straight up in the air. I sneezed violently, banging my head and momentarily losing my grip. I feared I would slip down the way I had come, but the cramped space aided in keeping a secure hold.

It was then that I understood the clue that McBride had provided Smith. Though able to wash up, McBride's constant sneezing into his black-stained handkerchief suggested to Smith that he had been underground recently and with some regularity as the dirt still filled his nasal passage. Ursula Trelawney's unknown exit from the antechamber on the second floor pointed to a secret passage in Redmoat. The very passage we were now scaling. McBride's involvement with Miss Trelawney made it elementary that if he had been underground, then it was reasonable to presume that he had used the same passage. My admiration for Smith knew no bounds. I would never have reached such a logical conclusion if left to my own devices.

The glare of the torch beam grew ever larger and I realized, with more than a bit of anxiety, that Smith had stopped moving forward. I feared he had run out of space and could either move no further or was unable to discover a means of releasing the latch that held us inside the passageway. I needn't have panicked. As I closed the gap between us, Smith shone the torch on his face so that I could see him clearly.

"This is it, Petrie. There is no way to know what is behind this door. Are you ready?"

I nodded yes. I couldn't bear another second in that cramped passageway than was absolutely necessary. If we stepped into the midst of the assembled hordes of Fu Manchu, it would have been preferable to another minute in that hellish dirt hole. Smith handed me the torch. I shone it on the wall in front of us and saw a handle and the clear outline of a door. Smith grasped the handle and nodded for me to extinguish the torch. Light flooded the passageway as Smith opened the door.

In a million years, I could not have imagined the unexpected sight which greeted our amazed eyes. Ursula Trelawney sat in a chair cradling what I at first took to be a child. Gradually, I realized it was the short, squat body of Neville McBride she held in her arms. The repulsive little toad of a man clung to her bosom as if he was an infant clutching to his doting wet nurse.

Ursula looked up at us and had the brazen audacity to actually smile. McBride's lips smacked loudly as his eyes flicked open. He turned and wiped a hand roughly across his saliva-smeared lips and bounded down from her lap. He started toward us with open arms.

"Mr. Smith! Dr. Petrie! At last, gentlemen, at last. I am pleased to say Eltham was right, you never disappoint. Never!"

My jaw hung slack. I was absolutely flabbergasted by this turn of events and questioned whether I was still under some twisted hypnotic spell.

"Come in, come in. I, of all people, know what a miserable place that tunnel is. You'll both need a bath, won't you? Ursula will be quite happy to bathe you."

Smith took his outstretched hand and climbed out of the oval mouth of the tunnel and stretched stiffly until he managed to stand on his own feet.

"No thank you, McBride. I am quite filthy as it is without having Miss Trelawney add to the feeling."

McBride clapped his hands together and laughed joyfully.

"Ever the outraged schoolmarm, eh, Mr. Smith? How delightful. Oh, I am so sorry, Dr. Petrie. Allow me."

He reached a hand out and hauled me from the mouth of the tunnel. My knees buckled and I grasped behind me for support. I gasped as I saw that obscene statue of the reclining nude likeness of Ursula Trelawney and realized that we had surfaced in the antechamber where the giant serpent had nearly killed Smith and me just a few short weeks before. The passageway was hidden at the base of the alabaster divan the statue rested upon. The door, invisible from the outside, had been designed, with the expected absence of taste, to open in the space just beneath the statue's spread-eagled legs.

McBride patted me down with both hands, doubtless checking to see if I was armed.

"There, see? Fit as a fiddle. A little... uh... a little climbing is good for one's health, I'm sure. Now, gentlemen, what can we do for you tonight, hmm?"

"You can start by answering a few questions, Mr. McBride," Smith snapped. "First of all, do you have in your possession a complete copy of Daniel Eltham's memoirs?"

McBride smiled and shook his head.

"No. I wish I did, truly. It would have saved us all a lot of bother."

"Second, was this secret passage used in the murder of Daniel Eltham?" Smith pointed toward the mouth of the entrance.

"Naturally, as was the passageway in my home in Dartford with the other five unfortunate victims. It made the transporting of bodies encased in snow possible. One couldn't reasonably be expected to pack corpses in snow in broad daylight, could one?"

I gasped in astonishment.

"So you admit to the murder of all six missionaries?"

McBride only chuckled. "Of course I admit to the murders, but don't make out as if it was accomplished in a single night. I'm not a madman, after all. We knew one of those six men had what we were looking for and, it was quite evident that whoever it was had no clue as to its true nature. Daniel was the most likely culprit and, as soon as we get our hands on that manuscript of his, we will be able to confirm this fact. I am afraid his daughter will have to be questioned and then disposed of as well. An unfortunate precautionary measure, but I trust you appreciate my position. One can never afford to be sloppy about witnesses, can one?"

"How were the missionaries killed?" I asked.

"Doctor, you disappoint me. I was expecting you would see right through that straight away being a medical man with some deductive ability, after all." He lowered his voice to a stage whisper. "I showed each of them the secret passageway. They were fascinated, but very dirty by the time they finished inspecting it. I poisoned the water they used to wash their faces. It caused a sudden fever and then they slipped into unconsciousness before death's rapid onset. I would have thought that irksome rash on their foreheads was a telltale sign for a medical man." He giggled like a child. "See? That was fairly obvious, was it? It's always best to do things the simple way. You'll find me an honest and forthright man on the best of occasions, gentlemen. What else can I tell you?"

"Have you and Thomas Valley truly ended your business partnership?" I asked.

"Ah, Dr. Petrie, I feared you might cross paths with Didimus at some point. I am afraid he is given to embellishing the facts to suit his whim of the moment."

"Didimus?"

"Oh, forgive me. Thomas means twin. Obviously you are not an Oxbridge man. In answer to your question, we have not. Thomas comes and goes as he pleases and leaves the daily grind of running the publishing company to me, but our partnership is as solid and true as it was the day we met… er, started. You'll forgive my slip of the tongue, I do hope."

"What connection exists between Esteban Milagro and Fulton Denison?" I demanded.

"Mr. Smith is very generous to allow you take the reins of the investigation like this, Dr. Petrie. I trust you appreciate your good fortune."

"Answer the question, McBride," Smith snapped with evident irritation.

"Well, that's a bit difficult. You see… Esteban Milagro was the founder of the Brotherhood of Magi. He died somewhere around 1715, I believe. Thomas took to adopting his identity some time ago. I should mention that Fulton Denison is another of Thomas' delightful little disguises. He has many of them, you know. Didimus, you see. Twin. He is Legion."

"He told us Prince Abard was Esteban Milagro!"

McBride laughed. "Oh my goodness, no. The man is incorrigible."

"Was Kane Keller another of the identities that Mr. Valley assumed?"

"Oh, Heavens! A thousand times, no! I know that man, Keller. He is an awful, vile, despicable person. Very, very unattractive. Although he has his uses." McBride smiled sheepishly. "He is a wonderful chemist. It was Keller who prepared the poisoned water for the missionaries. Yes, Kane can be the right man for the job when none other will do."

"Are you mad? I watched as Keenan Pethig died the most agonizingly painful death right before my eyes."

"My, you do get around, Doctor." McBride beamed at me. "All this dashing about clinging to Mr. Smith's coattails must have begun to rub off at last. Well done, man! Well done! You'd almost got the whole case sewn up all by yourself, hadn't you?"

I felt my blood boil. "Oh, I know it's all about that bloody signet ring if that's what you're getting at."

"Petrie, keep quiet, you fool!"

Smith's warning had come too late. McBride turned, eyes blazing, and grasped Ursula Trelawney by her left arm and dragged her bodily from the chair. She cried out for a moment, but he responded with a harsh slap across the side of her face. She fell with a whimper to the floor. McBride twisted her hair and roughly pulled her head backwards. He brandished a curved dagger and held it to her throat. I saw the point prick her neck. She drew her breath in with several pained gulps.

"Now, Doctor, you will hand over the Seal of Solomon or I'm afraid the floor is going to become awfully messy very, very quickly."

I reached into the breast pocket of my jacket and withdrew the Seal of Solomon. I had lied to Smith about losing it in Paris. It was mine to protect or dispose of as I saw fit. I held the ring in front of McBride's wide, staring eyes. That disturbing lopsided half-grin of his creased one side of his face as he gazed, transfixed at the object of his desire.

"Do you see it, my dear?" He spoke in hushed tones as he let go of her hair and removed the blade from her throat.

"I see it, my darling," she hissed. "The Sublime Black Prince will be pleased."

From her position on the floor, Ursula Trelawney's eyes were also fixated on the ring. The woman now looked positively feral. The two of them appeared bracing themselves to leap for my throat at any moment.

"Who the Hell is the Sublime Black Prince?" Smith growled.

McBride laughed cruelly.

"Don't mock those fools for their ignorance, Neville." Ursula clenched her fists as she spoke. "Tell them nothing. They will both die before morning. The whole world dies before morning."

McBride smiled. "One name is as good as another when one is immortal."

"We're not interested in your reincarnation rubbish, McBride, answer the question."

"Not reincarnation, you contemptible swine," McBride whispered in a soft voice. "Eternal life. The Sublime Black Prince cannot die any more than My Lady and I can. We serve the Old Ones and now, with that ring you possess, Dr. Petrie, the Seal shall be broken and the Old Ones will feast on the flesh of every man, woman, and child on this miserable little world. When the dawn breaks on a new day tomorrow, all life on this planet will be extinct."

"Then I had best hurry if I am to have the pleasure of killing you first."

At the unexpected sound of that powerful voice, the four of us spun toward the back of the room to see who had spoken. The door was open and the six snowmen we had seen in the Fox and Anchor stood silent and immobile. Standing at their side was an old man. A voice that could command nations had emerged from the bent, stooped form of an ancient Chinaman dressed in long-flowing yellow robes. A marmoset sat perched on his shoulder and chattered loudly as we stared, speechless at his unexpected arrival.

"Mr. McBride, Miss Trelawney," Smith's voice quivered as he spoke, "permit me to introduce... Dr. Fu Manchu."

## 25. THE RECKONING

"Dr. Petrie, your perseverance does credit to your race." Dr. Fu Manchu smiled as he spoke. "I did not anticipate ever seeing you again. Sadly, the fact remains that you and Nayland Smith are both fools for failing to heed my warning. It would have been better for you, Doctor, had you been devoured by my crocodile in Paris."

He hissed the name of that great city. His eyes glazed over as he spoke and that peculiar membrane that resembled a transparent eyelid descended over his pupils.

"You've been at the opium again, Doctor," Nayland Smith muttered underneath his breath.

The eyes of Fu Manchu flickered momentarily. The membrane receded, he blinked several times, and they returned to their catlike luminescence.

"You are an insolent cur and before you die, Nayland Smith," he purred as he pronounced his surname, "I shall have the pleasure of extracting the tongue from your mouth, personally."

Before he could make good on his threat, Neville McBride boldly stepped forward.

"It is a great honor to meet you face to face at last, Doctor." The little man beamed with all the demented glee he could muster. "The Brotherhood of Magi has long been looking forward to this day."

"The Brotherhood of Magi…" Fu Manchu extended the last syllable beyond recognition. "…have need of a new leader. Your Sublime Black Prince has paid the price for his indiscretions."

"What have you done to him?" Ursula cried out.

"Silence your whore, McBride, or I shall let my dacoits deal with her directly."

The six snowmen, having shed their featureless white-furred helmets and fur-covered gloves, stepped forward eagerly. Somehow, the combination of their tiny Oriental faces and hands contrasted with those monstrously large fur-covered suits leant the dacoits a queer mythological grace. McBride was grabbed by two of the snowmen, but offered no resistance.

Ursula Trelawney demonstrated her mastery of sleight of hand as they advanced. A fire appeared on the tip of her right index finger as if she were carrying a candle. Her hands were empty and yet the air was filled with the smell of sulphur. How she achieved such a feat was beyond my ken.

"What an amusing parlor trick, my dear," Fu Manchu's eyes disappeared as that loathsome smile split his face asunder. "Perhaps you would enjoy a little diversion of my own. I can remove both of your eyelids in but a few seconds using only my thumb and forefinger. Would you like to me to demonstrate?"

Ursula cowered on the floor and lowered her head like a dog that was reprimanded by the harsh tone in its master's voice.

"Who is this Sublime Black Prince they keep referring to?" I asked.

"I don't know, Petrie," Smith whispered. "Whoever it is, I don't think they're on our side."

Ursula held her arms aloft, crossed at the wrist with both her palms facing inward. As her hands slowly descended to rest upon her breasts, her face was obscured by a blue flame which hung magically in the air.

At a motion from their master's hand, one of the dacoits moved quickly and pinioned her arms behind her back. The blue flame dissipated into wisps of smoke. Ursula struggled momentarily, but it became clear the dacoit had overpowered her.

Fu Manchu shuffled up to her, leaning heavily on his wooden cane. He extended a bony hand and grasped her roughly by the chin, turning her head first left, then right.

"I know you, woman," he hissed. "I knew you years ago, when you were much older. You possess an elixir capable of rejuvenating the body until the decades fall away like leaves from a branch."

Ursula Trelawney held his stare and then spat at him. She said nothing, but she continued to glare at him contemptuously. Fu Manchu wiped his face with the sleeve of his robe and chuckled softly.

"Peko!"

At his master's command, the marmoset bounded from the doorway and leapt to his shoulder, chattering furiously all the while. Without so much as a gesture from Fu Manchu, the marmoset leaned forward and raked its claws across Ursula Trelawney's face. She screamed in pain. I saw her wince as a thin streak of crimson segmented her left eyelid. Her cheek had also been opened and was bleeding profusely.

"You fancy you can foretell the future, woman?" Fu Manchu's voice had switched to a nearly unintelligible guttural drone. "Now I shall tell you of what is to be your own future. I see you in the house of one of my friends. A great marquis in Japan. He has you tied to the rack and is using the ancient methods of teaching a woman the measure of respect she should have for her master. You shall learn the point where pain and pleasure are obscured as you receive the gift of total freedom from sensation. There is only the eternal sting and the knowledge that comfort and peace are things of the past. Take her from me and let her contemplate her fate."

He whirled suddenly as the dacoit dragged Ursula Trelawney kicking and screaming from the room. Fu Manchu hobbled over to where McBride was being held. The little man looked absolutely terrified.

"You... you killed Thomas?" he blubbered.

Fu Manchu regarded him for a moment.

"He is not... dead," Dr. Fu Manchu responded, choosing his words with great deliberation. "The man you call Thomas Valley has been removed like the thorn from the lion's paw. He has been cast aside. He aspired to rise to a seat among the Council of Seven. He dared to challenge me, hoping to supplant me, dreaming to steal my destiny. I who command the powers of darkness. He, a miserable little Englishman lusting for glory." His voice had risen to manic heights as he spoke.

"He had a weakness, a fondness that proved easy to exploit." Fu Manchu's voice was soft, almost gentle. I quivered as I thought of whom he was speaking. "He shall find his appetite not so easily sated in the future. There are not many... eh, companions... interested in sharing the company of a man whose mouth has been carved into a permanent leer."

Neville McBride's face was covered in perspiration. He shook visibly and uttered an obscenity.

"There is the matter now, Mr. McBride, of repaying the debt that you owe to the Si-Fan," Dr. Fu Manchu stressed each vowel as he spoke in a soft purr.

"What debt? I... I don't know what you are talking about," McBride sputtered.

The many lines that encircled Fu Manchu's aged face broke into a smile that held no mirth. Eyes shone that knew no joy and no mercy.

"The debt is one you will recall presently, I assure you. You paid a man in Limehouse for the use of Chinese girls for an evening's diversion. Wal Tam had no right to barter with you. Before he died, he informed his executioner that he made it abundantly clear the girls were not to be compromised. You defied these instructions. You could have paid far less for any number of women whose innocence was not measured beyond worldly riches. You chose not to because the very act of defiling the innocent was important for the ritual conducted by your Brethren that evening. Wal Tam has paid the penalty for his transgression. Now you shall do the same."

A dacoit approached and pinioned McBride's arms behind his back. The miserable little man made no attempt to resist. Resting an elbow on the wooden cane while another dacoit steadied him, Dr. Fu Manchu grasped McBride's head between his two bony hands and squeezed until the little man's face began to redden from the pressure exerted by those unnaturally powerful hands. McBride shook, convulsively. His sweat-streaked face resembled an overripe melon covered in fresh morning dew. His teeth ground into one another as he struggled to weather the pain. Amazingly, he made no sound.

Dr. Fu Manchu suddenly jerked McBride's head to the left and, with a terrible snap; released the head from his grasp and let it fall limp and unseeing against the man's now lifeless body.

"It is finished." Dr. Fu Manchu bowed reverently as he spoke. "Neville McBride lacked the imagination to elevate himself above the status of the degenerate toad. May he return as one in his next life."

Strange as it may now seem, Nayland Smith and I made no move to escape or intervene. We stood rooted to the spot. My mind reeled as I tried to take in all that I had seen and heard.

"Thomas... Thomas Valley was the Sublime Black Prince?"

Nayland Smith shot me a glance as I stammered my question.

Dr. Fu Manchu turned towards our direction once more and smiled.

"Do you find the notion so impossible to accept, Dr. Petrie?"

I was nearly speechless and fought to control my tongue.

"I... I understand the man was... well... it's hard to imagine he was at the heart of this business and not just a... I mean to say he seemed so... so..."

"Respectable?" Fu Manchu pronounced the word with mocking sincerity. "You have not lived long enough yet to learn what lies beneath the sheen of respectability. The lot of them were fools. Where are they now? Headless, maimed, chained, and dead. Scattered to the four winds. Scheming fools who sought a power that was beyond their abilities to wield. You will give me the ring now, Dr. Petrie."

He held his hand out as if speaking to a child. I started. I had not anticipated this command.

"Do as he says, Petrie," Nayland Smith prodded me. "These are not the odds to gamble against."

I reached into the breast pocket of my jacket and withdrew the signet ring. I thought of all that had transpired on its journey from the poor bonze's pagoda to this day in Redmoat where it now rested in the palm of Fu Manchu's hand. The Devil Doctor held the ring as if it were the most precious treasure in the world. I thought of Prince Abard's words of superstition and dread. Why did these men afford this simple object such reverence?

"Ready the altar!" Dr. Fu Manchu shouted triumphantly.

The five remaining snowmen approached the alabaster divan where Ursula's marble likeness was carved. As one, the dacoits pressed against the statue until it toppled sideways and shattered with a terrible crash. I looked upon the base of the statue in amazement. The divan was now gone and in its place was revealed a stone altar. The same altar I had seen in Paris when Thomas Valley initiated me and Gaston Max into the Brotherhood of Magi. The same altar I had seen in the drawings hidden in the chest in Kane Keller's apartment. The same altar I had seen depicted in Esteban Milagro's book at the Bibliothèque Nationale. Now, the very same sacrificial altar was revealed to be in Redmoat.

I knew our fates were sealed, but I did not want to die. I wanted to live. I wanted Kara. I wanted to marry her and raise a family. There were so many things I had yet to accomplish.

"Dr. Fu Manchu!"

I called out his name. The frail-looking Chinaman turned to face me.

"I offer you my liberty and loyalty in exchange for Kara's freedom. Let her go. She has served you faithfully."

"Petrie!" Smith cried out, aghast. "Have you gone mad?"

Dr. Fu Manchu threw back his head and laughed. The sound was harsh and cold.

"Fear not, Mr. Smith. I have no intention of losing so valuable a servant as Karamaneh. Your liberty is not yours to bargain with, Dr. Petrie. Nonetheless, I graciously accept your offer of serving me—if only this one last time. The Seal of Solomon requires careful handling. I have no desire of risking my own life in summoning demons when it is far simpler to expend yours."

Dr. Fu Manchu gestured and Smith and I were both taken and bound by dacoits. Smith was thrown roughly to the floor whilst I was herded, like a lamb, before the altar. Dr. Fu Manchu stood before me. Presently, he turned and addressed me.

"The Evil that is held in check by the Seal of Solomon is too strong to resist for all but the chaste and holy. A combination not easily found amongst the Brotherhood of Magi. That is why they were doomed to fail. I had intended that Greba Eltham fulfill this role of honor, but you saw to that by interfering with my plans and robbing her of her virtue. It would be quite unfortunate if Karamaneh ever learned of this little indiscretion of yours, Doctor. I fear it would be more than her delicate nature could handle. She gives her body so willingly for the Si-Fan, but reserves her heart just for you. Knowledge of such a trifling thing such as this would surely destroy her. I wonder... do you think that she would throw herself into her work with greater abandon if she were aware of your cruel and callous betrayal of her love?"

I strained against my bonds to no avail. I wanted to strangle him. I hated him for I knew he spoke the truth.

"Denis Nayland Smith could never be trusted with the task at hand. That leaves you as the most viable candidate, Dr. Petrie. You are lacking in faith and integrity, but these are requisite qualities only when one is trying to save the vessel's soul. Once you have summoned the demons, they can pull the bones from your still breathing chest and feast upon your heart. It matters not what is done with you for you will have fulfilled your purpose for the Si-Fan. A far greater purpose than you were born for, I daresay. "

"You're mad!" I shouted back at him. "You really believe this demon nonsense? It's folklore, Doctor. Surely, a man of your intelligence and education can appreciate that simple fact."

"You know I am not a religious man, Petrie, but the Si-Fan would not have invested their time and energy if there were nothing to these claims." Smith's usually tanned features looked pale and drawn as he shouted from the floor of the altar. "Whatever this ring is capable of doing means destruction on a mass scale for England and possibly the entire world. Do not take this lightly. Use me as your vessel, Fu Manchu. I give you my word that I will not betray you."

Dr. Fu Manchu chuckled softly. That mummified face came alive once more as his eyes burned like coals in their sockets.

"Oh, Mr. Smith, I do not give you enough credit. You are most dangerous when you are desperate. You resemble the cornered mongoose even now. I know better than to trust such a man with the power to destroy me. You are too strong-willed and you present no bargaining chip such as Karamaneh to still your hand should you gain the advantage. You will be of no use to my purpose save to help stave off the demon's hunger. No, it is Dr. Petrie I want and it is he that I shall have."

A short time later, I found myself still bound, but now dressed in a white tunic. Two of the dacoits lifted me up and laid me across the altar. My ankles were then likewise bound. I knew not what to expect. Dr. Fu Manchu stood by my side, both hands supporting his weight as he leaned against the altar. His eyes had taken on that queer opaque quality once more. His irises had clouded over, nearly obscured by that milky film. He appeared to be in a state of great contemplation. Finally, the clouds dispersed and those iridescent cat-green eyes shone through once more.

"You shall bear the Seal of Solomon, Dr. Petrie," he said in a commanding tone.

The signet ring was resting on a small pillow. Fu Manchu gently lowered the pillow and placed it on my chest. I did not believe anything supernatural would occur. I was doomed to die in some mindless Pagan ritual. Another wasted life sacrificed to the empty Heavens.

Dr. Fu Manchu raised his arms in prayer and began speaking in some long forgotten tongue. Gradually, I found that I was able to understand parts of what he said, although I was certain he was not speaking English.

*"Long protected by the Lamas of Rache Churan, we bring forth the Seal of Solomon once again and call upon the great and terrible Asmodeus. We command you, Asmodeus, to awaken from your aeons-long slumber to feast upon the creatures of this world once more!"*

The room was plunged in near total darkness now apart from the candles the dacoits had arranged about the altar. They flickered briefly as a chill wind moved around me where I lay. As I watched in disbelief, the candles gave off a pungent odor and a thick, yellow smoke poured forth from them. The smoke seemed to merge just above me and obscured my view of the signet ring resting on my chest. Slowly, the smoke began to coalesce and a figure began to take shape within its vapors.

The color of the smoke started to fade as the figure took on the likeness of… I doubted my sanity, but the likeness of a horned snow beast. Foul-smelling white smoke poured upward as the details of the creature's form took shape. The smoke began to build steadily as the creature seemed to fill the entire room.

My heart was racing. There was no rational explanation for what I had seen. I lost all awareness of Fu Manchu. I could not see him or hear his voice. I saw only that monstrous shape at once reminiscent of the snowman that concealed Eltham's dead body and of the suits worn by the dacoits. Was this the legendary Yeti of Tibetan lore?

I struggled to shake my head, but I could not clear the vision from my eyes. This must be some effect of the opiate burning in the dragon-headed briars. This could not be reality. The monstrous form grew larger by the second until it filled the entire area of the room with its gigantic girth.

I watched in sickening fascination as a fissure erupted just above the creature's loins. The fissure widened and a darkness could be seen behind the crack as it spread, tearing through the smoke with unbelievable speed. As the fissure reached the snow creature's throat, the horned head appeared to bend backwards and twist. Grey tendrils began to flail about within the fissure… no, not tendrils, entrails were pouring forth. There were tens of thousands of undulating mucous-coated entrails winding about one another. I realized, to my horror, that the smoke-filled snow creature was no more, and in its place stood a massive amalgamation of writhing, billowing entrails eagerly reaching for my flesh.

"*Hear me, Asmodeus!*"

Dr. Fu Manchu's voice rang out all around me though his lips did not part.

"*I command you through this vessel that has opened the Seal that held you captive through the millennia. Give me the power to enslave this world! Release all of the ancient evils upon the coming century. War, hate, fear, desperation, injustice, cruelty, cowardice! I name you, Asmodeus. Take root in the souls of the kingdoms of this world. Bring its miserable people to their knees. Let their accomplishments grow as their humanity diminishes. Let them topple and fall and descend into barbarism once more. Heed my plea and grant me this boon!"*

I understood now. This was Evil personified before my eyes. I saw the blade of the dagger glittering above me. I could not see Dr. Fu Manchu's bony hand, yet I knew his fingers were wrapped about its hilt. My blood would open the Seal and allow these atrocities to be visited upon the world. I was the lamb waiting to be sacrificed upon the altar. Imperfect as I was, I was the vessel by which the world would be plunged into darkness and doom.

I saw the blade flash downwards. The fire in my brain had become an incessant pounding. I felt as if a mallet were hammering against my skull. The drumming resounded again and again in my mind.

*Bismillah. Bismillah. Bismillah. Bismillah. Bismillah. Bismillah. Bismillah.*

I was confronted with Evil as a supernatural entity. Evil made manifest as a swirling mass of bloody entrails before me. If Evil could exist in such a form, there had to be Good. It was only rational. It was our only hope. It was all that could save me. It was all that could save Smith or Kara or anyone in this world.

*Christ! God! Let me believe in you. Protect me. Safeguard me. Spare me from this fate. I believe in your Goodness. Free me from this sorry plight.*

Before I could finish my awkward, half-believing prayer, lightning struck and thunder crashed around me as two powerful hands grasped my arms and pulled me backwards off of the altar. As I was pulled clear, I saw the blade strike downwards towards my chest, but I knew no pain.

"Thank God, Smith! You're free! You saved me!" I cried.

I could still feel the firm grip on my arms. I glanced back and the hairs on my neck rose. None stood behind me and yet I could still feel the strength of the grip upon my arms, supporting my weight as I hung limply on my feet.

I whimpered like a child. If this was faith, I wanted no part of it. Leave me in my blissful doubting ignorance. Don't make me acknowledge such madness as reality.

My hands burned with pain. I dropped the signet ring to the floor and kicked at it, hatefully. How it came to be in my hands again I knew not. I glanced to the altar where it had rested on the pillow and saw the tip of the dagger embedded in the pillow's very center. All around me was that pungent yellow smoke. The undulating, slime-covered entrails had disappeared. The Seal was shut and could not be re-opened. Fu Manchu had failed.

A blood-curdling cry tore me from my jumbled thoughts. Fu Manchu was wailing, arms held aloft.

"No!" he shrieked. "I will not be undone. Not when I have come so close. The power was within my grasp. Time is my enemy. A single lifetime is insufficient to achieve my ambitions. I will not be denied! All of my work... all of my years of planning... undone by the pointless machinations of a self-serving, traitorous fool."

He collapsed upon the ground. I could hear his wheezing breath, gasping for air. I was struggling to steady my shaken nerves. As I glanced about the room, I saw the five remaining snowmen, lying spread-eagled upon the stone floor. Their faces and hands were blackened as if they had been struck by the lightning that had flashed around me mere moments before.

"What happened, Petrie? What was that thing?"

Nayland Smith struggled to speak as he lay upon his side on the floor in front of the altar.

"It was the solution to the churchman's dilemma."

No sooner had I spoken than a thunderclap shook the room and the altar burst into flames. The fire quickly spread to the carpet.

"Hurry, Petrie, before it is too late!" Smith cried.

I leapt down from the altar and quickly undid his bonds. He rubbed his wrists for a moment and then we ran for the door.

"They're locked!" I shouted.

"The dacoits, Fu Manchu, McBride... one of them must have the keys!"

I rushed to the first of the dead snowmen and pulled at his fur-covered waist. The suit appeared to cover the entire body. No join was visible. I gagged at the smell of his charred, blackened flesh. The billowing smoke from the spreading fire was beginning to fill my lungs. I rolled his body over and tore at the stitching at the back of his suit. I worked frantically and ripped the fabric apart until I came to the belt upon his waist. A set of keys jangled on a ring. I tugged at the ring until they snapped free.

The fire was raging all around us. We had come so far and survived so much to die in blazing flames seemed impossibly cruel. Little air remained in the smoke-filled room. I threw Smith the keys as he started for the doorway. I knelt before Fu Manchu. Despite all that he had done, I could not leave him to die in the flames. I wrestled with the thought that he deserved to be left to his fate.

A fate Smith and I may yet share, I thought, as the ceiling began to collapse around us. Fu Manchu let out a terrible cry. A burning roof beam had fallen across his crippled form. I bent to lift it, but snatched back my hands from the heat. There would be no escape for the Devil Doctor this time. A glowing ember caught my eye. *No not an ember,* I thought as I reached down to pluck my prize from the ground.

"Hurry, Petrie. We cannot wait any longer."

Nayland Smith reached out a hand and pulled me away. Together, we rushed for the stairs. The flames had reached the first level. Smoke was everywhere. Redmoat was collapsing all around us. We reached the first level and ran as if the very fires of Hell were at our feet.

We did not cease running until we had broken into the surrounding shrubbery. There was an enormous wrenching sound. We looked with horror as the front of Redmoat's very structure collapsed, still burning, into the empty moat. The snow-covered shrubs and cabbage plants would contain the fire's wrath, but the smoke would remain thick and impenetrable for many hours.

"Is it over?" I asked Smith, choking back tears. "Is Dr. Fu Manchu finally dead?"

Smith did not answer me. We could not dare believe he was gone until we examined his charred and smoking remains. Smith was coughing violently. I patted him on the back and suggested we keep moving. I looked up at the rising sun in the sky and smiled.

"Happy Christmas, Smith." I said.

## 26. CODA

There is little more to tell of our adventure. The evening of the last day of 1913 found Smith and I ensconced in the apartments he leased from Colonel Bickerstaff. I closed my hollowed-out copy of the King James Bible after placing the last few pages of my account of the Six Snowmen and the terrible fate that threatened Ursula Trelawney inside it.

I did not think I would ever submit this particular tale to *The Story-Teller* for publication. The details were too personal and the events too shocking to share with the public. Likewise I made the decision, for right or for wrong, to burn Eltham's manuscript. I never read a single word more than I had read on my return from Paris. Eltham's madness had poisoned too many lives. There was no need to prolong his influence.

Greba never read her father's book, gratefully. It was better now that she would never have the opportunity. She was able to return to London, all threat of the Si-Fan and anyone else foolish enough to seek for the Seal of Solomon having been removed. My relationship with her would never be the same. Although Kara was still little more than a memory who haunted my days and nights, she was also the only woman I would ever love. I knew that now. I also realized I was unworthy of her love, but that was my burden to bear.

Gaston Max's reputation continued to grow and his fame spread well beyond Paris. He never told me whether he considered me a scorpion or a frog. He didn't need to. I knew what I had been and I knew the power to change was within my grasp.

I often found myself thinking of Kau. He had risked his very life to try to help Greba and me to escape I regretted having misjudged him for no better reason than his race and his disfigurement. He was both noble and courageous. He was a Chinaman, a member of the Si-Fan, and he was my better.

I would never know if Eltham's ghost had really given me that icon and taught me the meaning of the Arabic word *Bismillah*, or if there was some rational explanation. The man I knew as Thomas Valley and Dr. Fu Manchu were both powerful mesmerists and either certainly had the ability to deceive me into thinking they were Eltham's spirit, but for what purpose? It was a mystery that would remain unanswered... in this life.

The questions surrounding the final fate of the Si-Fan's most dangerous agent was resolved sooner than I would have liked. Just after we returned from our final dinner of the year at the Fox and Anchor, Smith shared a telegram with me that had arrived earlier in the day. He had not wished to spoil my appetite by disclosing its contents sooner. I picked up the telegram and sat by the fire to read it.

*I SURVIVED THE FLAMES. STOP. THE TRAITOR YET LIVES. STOP. SEEK NOT MY ASHES LEST YOU BE BURNED. STOP.*

The telegram was unsigned. No signature was necessary.

"Do you believe that Dr. Fu Manchu's survival indicates that Asmodeus' curse of war, hate, and fear has been loosed upon the world in this next century? Is there no hope for mankind?" I asked Smith.

He shrugged and puffed at his pipe as he looked outside at the yellow moon that hung above us in the clear night sky.

"Who can say, Petrie? 1914 is upon us. Let us see what the New Year brings."

I reflected on that very subject and would have sworn the warm glow from the signet ring hidden in my breast pocket intensified ever so slightly while I was lost in my hopes and fears for the future.

## THE END

# BLACK COAT PRESS

M. Allain & P. Souvestre. *The Daughter of Fantômas*
Anicet-Bourgeois. *Rocambole*
Guy d'Armen. *Doc Ardan: The City of Gold and Lepers*
Aloysius Bertrand. *Gaspard de la Nuit*
A. Bisson & G. Livet. *Nick Carter vs. Fantômas*
Félix Bodin. *The Novel of the Future*
Lucien Dabril. *Rocambole*
V. Darlay & H. de Gorsse. *Lupin vs. Holmes: The Stage Play*
C.I. Defontenay. *Star (Psi Cassiopeia)*
Charles Derennes: *The People of the Pole*
Alexandre Dumas. *The Return of Lord Ruthven*
J.-C. Dunyach. *The Night Orchid: Conan Doyle in Toulouse*
Paul Féval: *Anne of the Isles*
Paul Féval. *The Blackcoats: The Companions of the Treasure*
Paul Féval. *The Blackcoats: The Invisible Weapon*
Paul Féval. *The Blackcoats: The Parisian Jungle*
Paul Féval. *The Blackcoats: 'Salem Street*
Paul Féval. *Captain Phantom*
Paul Féval. *Gentlemen of the Night*
Paul Féval. *John Devil*
Paul Féval. *Knightshade*
Paul Féval. *Revenants*
Paul Féval. *Vampire City*
Paul Féval. *The Vampire Countess*
Paul Féval. *The Wandering Jew's Daughter*
Paul Féval, *fils. Felifax, the Tiger-Man*
Arnould Galopin. *Doctor Omega*
V. Hugo, Foucher & Meurice. *The Hunchback of Notre-Dame*
O. Joncquel & Theo Varlet. *The Martian Epic*
Jean de La Hire. *The Nyctalope on Mars*
Jean de La Hire. *The Nyctalope vs. Lucifer*
Steve Leadley. *Sherlock Holmes - The Circle of Blood*
Maurice Leblanc. *Lupin vs. Holmes: The Hollow Needle*
Maurice Leblanc. *Lupin vs. Holmes: The Blonde Phantom*
Gustave Le Rouge. *The Vampires of Mars*

Gaston Leroux. *Chéri-Bibi*
Gaston Leroux. *The Phantom of the Opera*
Jean-Marc Lofficier. *The Katrina Protocol*
Jean-Marc & Randy Lofficier. *Edgar Allan Poe on Mars*
Jean-Marc & Randy Lofficier. *Robonocchio*
Lofficier. *Tales of the Shadowmen 1: The Modern Babylon*
Lofficier. *Tales of the Shadowmen 2: Gentlemen of the Night*
Lofficier. *Tales of the Shadowmen 3: Danse Macabre*
Lofficier. *Tales of the Shadowmen 4: Lords of Terror*
Lofficier. *Tales of the Shadowmen 5: The Vampires of Paris*
Xavier Mauméjean. *The League of Heroes*
William Patrick Maynard. *The Terror of Fu Manchu*
Frank J. Morlock. *Sherlock Holmes: The Grand Horizontals*
Marie Nizet. *Captain Vampire*
C. Nodier, Beraud & Toussaint-Merle. *Frankenstein*
Charles Nodier. *Lord Ruthven the Vampire*
Henri de Parville. *An Inhabitant of the Planet Mars*
John William Polidori. *Lord Ruthven the Vampire*
P.-A. Ponson du Terrail. *The Vampire and the Devil's Son*
Albert Robida. *The Clock of the Centuries*
Eugène Scribe. *Lord Ruthven the Vampire*
Brian Stableford. *The Germans on Venus*
Brian Stableford. *News from the Moon*
Brian Stableford. *The New Faust at the Tragicomique*
Brian Stableford. *The Shadow of Frankenstein*
Brian Stableford. *Sherlock Holmes - The Vampires of Eternity*
Brian Stableford. *The Stones of Camelot*
Brian Stableford. *The Wayward Muse*
Villiers de l'Isle-Adam. *The Scaffold*
Villiers de l'Isle-Adam. *The Vampire Soul*
Philippe Ward. *Artahe: The Legacy of Jules de Grandin*
P. de Wattyne & Y. Walter. *Sherlock Holmes vs. Fantômas*
David White: *Fantômas in America*

Milton Keynes UK
Ingram Content Group UK Ltd.
UKHW011301031023
429867UK00001B/13